The Sicilian's Forgotten Wife

Alexia Adams

Copyright

The Sicilian's Forgotten Wife
(previously published as Under the Sicilian Sky)
By Alexia Adams
Copyright © 2017 by Alexia Adams

Published by:
Alexia Adams
Suite 377
255 Newport Drive
Port Moody, BC V3H 5H1
Canada

Contact: Alexia@alexia-adams.com
www.alexia-adams.com

Edited by Julie Sturgeon
Cover design by Katie Kenyhercz

Print ISBN 978-1-9991756-2-7
e-ISBN 978-1-9991756-0-3

Second Print Edition September 2019

This story was originally published December 2017
By Crimson Romance (an imprint of Simon &
Schuster)
with the title
Under the Sicilian Sky

Dedication

I dedicate this book to Benedict Cumberbatch. He knows why.

Chapter One

Mario bit back the angry words at the tip of his tongue. Venting might make him feel better, but it wouldn't fix the problem. "This load isn't secured properly," he said to the driver in Arabic.

The driver tugged on one of the ropes as if to prove it was stable, and the load shifted farther to the left.

"Stop!" Mario yelled. This shipment of sunbaked clay vases was already two days late. If it didn't get to the port in time to load on the boat to Rotterdam, all their diligent planning to ensure his company's perfect supply record would be ruined. More importantly, it would delay construction of the medical facility that would provide much-needed healthcare for the women who made the vases.

Before Mario could instruct the driver on how to tie down the crates properly, a bell sounded and the village's newly built school let out. Within seconds, he was surrounded by children of all different sizes. Eighteen months ago, when he'd first come to this Libyan village, the specter of death had hung low over the mud and straw huts. Now the laughter of children competed with the women's songs as they worked at

1

something that earned them a decent living. If he accomplished nothing else in his life, he could say he'd helped save these precious humans from malnourishment.

"Super Mario, Super Mario," the children chanted as he handed out colored pencils. It never ceased to amaze him that kids on the edge of the Sahara, who had little contact with the outside world, had heard of the game after which he was named. Or renamed, as the case was. His last name, Barilla, he'd taken off a package of pasta. He dreamed in Italian, so he figured that must be his native language and nationality. But no male matching his description had been reported missing in Italy. So, really, it was anyone's guess where he'd come from.

A loud *creak* from the crates perched precariously on the truck brought his attention back to the load of precious cargo. He couldn't allow three months' worth of the women's hard work to be destroyed because one man was too lazy or too stupid to do his job properly.

"Go now," he told the children. "I'll come say goodbye in a minute."

With the colored pencils clutched in their little hands, they raced off to show their mothers what he'd brought this time. Farrah had a small girl on each of her hips, one barely old enough to walk. The smile on his business partner's face as she watched the others race off was one of pure delight. She adored children.

He and Farrah had the same goals and work ethic and enjoyed each other's company. More than once he'd considered transitioning their working relationship to include a personal one. But the golden shackle on his ring finger told him he was in no position to offer her marriage.

The driver moved to the other side of the vehicle and tugged on the rope across the top of the cargo. The uppermost crate slid closer to the edge, barely supported now by the one below it. Mario's heart froze as he calculated the trajectory should it fall—straight on top of Farrah and the baby girls.

"Farrah! Move!" Mario screamed. As though in slow motion, she looked up, her eyes widening and, mouth open, tried to hurry away. But her foot caught on her long skirt, pitching her forward. He raced to her side, his movements slowed by the loose sand under his feet. Heart in his throat, he managed to catch her and the two toddlers she held.

A loud *snap*. The top crate teetered then tumbled. He swiveled, placing himself between the falling cargo and Farrah and the two children. A scream. A sharp burst of intense brightness, like a star going supernova. Then everything went black.

"Mario, Mario!" A frantic voice came to him through the dark. Something touched his face and he went to move his head but stopped at the searing pain.

He tried to open his eyes, but a blinding light made him close them again.

"He's coming around," another voice added.

The sunshine penetrating his eyelids dimmed and he made another attempt to open them.

"Mario, are you okay?"

He turned toward the voice and darkness descended again for a second. When he managed to focus, the face of a beautiful woman with dark, kohl-

3

rimmed eyes, wearing a white hijab, greeted him. His brain searched for a name. Bella? No. Farrah.

"I'm okay." His lips were covered in sand, and as he spoke some fell in his mouth. He tried to spit it out, but he was too dry.

"Can he sit up?" Farrah asked the UN healthcare worker who knelt on his other side.

"Yes, I don't think anything is broken," the man replied. "But he should get to a city and have that head wound checked out. He probably has a concussion."

Farrah handed him a bottle of water while she propped him up against her. He closed his eyes as the world spun.

"What happened?"

"The top crate fell off the truck and hit you on the head," she answered.

"Is Bella okay?" he asked.

"Bella?" Farrah's brows drew together, and she exchanged a worried look with the doctor.

A flood of pictures swamped his mind. His wife. His father. Sicily. The farm. Smiling down at a dark-haired woman as they exchanged vows on the beach. Her gorgeous hazel eyes were lit with happiness, her small, delicate hand holding his, trusting him, loving him, as he slid a wedding ring on her finger.

"I remember." He wanted to shout for joy but his head objected. Instead he grabbed Farrah's hand and squeezed it tight. "My name is Matteo Vanni. I lived on a farm in Sicily with my father and wife Bella." He tried to sit up but slumped back as a wave of pain overwhelmed him.

"Mario?" A tear glistened in the corner of her eye.

4

He softened his tone and attempted a reassuring smile. "Don't you see, Farrah, this is the break I need. I remember who I am, where I've come from. Knowing my past, I can fix the things that have stopped me from claiming a future."

A spark of optimism warmed her gaze as it roved over his features. "You mean, after all these years, we may finally be able to do more than make other people's dreams come true?" She brushed a lock of his hair off his forehead, her fingers lingering in the touch.

"That's my hope. I just need a few weeks to sort out whatever is left of my life in Sicily."

He could find out why his wife hadn't bothered to file a missing persons report when he disappeared. Then he could get rid of this band that bound him to a woman who obviously didn't care enough to even look for him.

Dio, what if she'd been involved in the accident that claimed his memory and left him near dead, washed up on a Tunisian beach in only his underpants?

At least now he knew where to get answers to the myriad of questions that kept him awake at night. He was going back to Sicily.

***

Bella tugged her gray knee-length shift dress over her head. Here I go again. Attempt to have a personal life, take ten. A small glass of wine right now held real appeal. Or maybe a large glass and she could call a taxi. This was completely ridiculous. Why should this date be any different from the previous nine? They'd all ended in disappointment, and this one didn't even have the 'friend of a friend' criteria.

Her first internet date. Maybe an impartial algorithm would have more luck finding a suitable man for her. Problem was, they were all technically suitable, except those who were only after her land. They just weren't Matteo. After six months of finally getting back into the dating scene, she still compared every man to her husband. Missing husband. Dead husband.

She'd spent the first two years of his disappearance in denial, expecting him to come through the door any second while worrying that the rumors about him were true. Then another year had passed while she'd attempted to remove all trace of him from her life, shredding the clothes of the bastard who had abandoned her with his sick father and failing farm. Bargaining with the universe for Matteo's safe return had been a waste of time, but, still, she'd done that for six months. Depression had swallowed up another year. According to the grief cycle, she should now be in acceptance mode.

She was doing her damnedest to move on. But sometimes, like today, she was back at square one. Hopefully, if she had to go through the process again, anger wouldn't be too long in coming.

She got a lot done when she was mad.

Emptiness threatened to consume her again and she rushed from the bedroom. She was tired of being alone. Tired of having no one to share her life with, to laugh with, to snuggle with on a cold winter night. Tired of fighting all the battles by herself. She was twenty-eight and felt eighty-two.

Dutch courage would have to wait. She grabbed her handbag and keys and headed out to a new-to-her Fiat 500. At least she was fairly certain it would get her to her destination. Her old farm truck was more cantankerous than the ram she brought in to service her ewes. God, even her sheep had sex more regularly than she did.

Her phone pinged with an incoming message. Maybe her date was canceling and she could stay home and get friendly with a bottle of wine.

Sorry, Bella. Urgent meeting has come up. I may not make it to Sicily after all.

Not her date, just a text from Kai Andersen, her ex-fiancé, the man she'd left so she could marry Matteo. Despite their broken engagement, they'd remained friends. A consultant to Doctors Without Borders, Kai was in Europe and had said he'd stop by to see her before returning to New York. Now she didn't even have his visit to look forward to.

Butterflies swarmed in her stomach as she parked near the restaurant where she was to meet her internet date. In the small Sicilian village, where everyone knew everyone, it was hard to find someone who was willing to take a chance on the crazy American girl who drove her husband to disappear and then buried her father-in-law three years later. But at least she'd progressed from being called "Matteo's wife" to "Matteo's widow" to "Signora Bella Vanni, owner of Vanni Farms." Her date came from three towns away.

Sufficient distance that, if tonight didn't go well, she wouldn't constantly run into him.

It took two tries before she could force her hand to the door pull. *Come on, Bella. You can do this.* The hostess showed her to a table for two, and Bella deliberately chose the chair facing away from the front so she wouldn't stare at it and talk herself out of this stupid idea.

A short, stocky man slid into the chair opposite and held out his hand. "Signora Bella, you are even more beautiful than your photo." First mistake, reminding her she was married. Her thumb automatically rubbed the spot where her ring used to sit—the long-gone symbol of a love she should have stopped clinging to years ago.

Bella forced a smile and took the man's meaty hand in hers. It was a limp shake, like holding a dead fish. Her date had small, beady eyes and had already licked his lips three times in the two seconds since he'd sat down. Too bad she couldn't say the same about his photo versus reality. There should be a private hell for people who Photoshopped their online dating profile picture. She held back the deep sigh that threatened to escape. This was such a mistake.

The creepy feeling of being watched crawled up her back as she walked from the restaurant to the car two hours later. Yet despite looking around, she couldn't spot anyone. *Come on, don't get paranoid. This is village life. By dawn everyone will know I've had yet another unsuccessful date.*

She pulled up in front of her tiny house and slumped in her seat. Gino or Gianni, whatever his name was, had been okay in the end. He'd been intelligent, interested in her businesses and plans for expansion, even offered a few helpful suggestions. But there'd been no spark. The plump, slightly damp lips he'd pressed against her cheek as they'd said goodnight had made her shudder. She'd tried to disguise it as a shiver of cold, but as it was nearly seventy-five degrees, even at ten p.m., that hadn't cut it. They'd left with an, "I'll call you," promise, which meant that neither would. And she wasn't disappointed.

Matteo, you left a hell of a legacy. Even six years later, she clenched her pelvic muscles when she remembered his loving. God, he'd been a fantastic kisser, and that had nothing on the magic his hands created, caressing her skin, sliding his strong fingers into her heat...

Damn, it was going to be one of those nights. She pulled the keys from the ignition and was about to get out of the car when headlights blinded her through her rearview mirror. She had locked the gate after she'd come through, hadn't she? Living alone, so far from any neighbors, she was aware of how vulnerable she was. Should she run to the house and get the shotgun, or stay within the protection of her car so she could drive away if need be? Her muscles coiled and the heat of her earlier thoughts was replaced by cold, hard fear.

The vehicle rolled closer, finally parking next to hers. Glancing over, her breath whooshed out. It was Cristoforo. Of course, he had a key to the gate. Her husband's best friend had been a rock since her father-in-law's death.

She slipped from her car and met him at the front

door.

"I wanted to make sure you got home okay," he said. "And find out how it went." He shrugged as if slightly embarrassed.

"It was fine. But I won't be seeing him again. Come in for a glass of wine. How was your trip to Milan?" She unlocked the door and flipped on the lights. Her stone-walled cottage was tiny but cool in summer and warm in winter.

"Boring. Banking is not as exciting as it may appear," he said with a laugh. "You sit, I'll get the wine. Then I want all the juicy details, girlfriend." He put on a mock American accent, and Bella laughed again.

Cristo was … comfortable. He'd seen her at her worst, so there was no need to pretend she was anything special. He'd recently turned down an amazing promotion opportunity at the bank because he needed to take care of his aging parents. In America, he'd have been called a menopause baby, conceived when his mother had given up any hope of having a child. Here in Sicily, it was called a miracle.

He strode into the living room with two glasses and a bottle of red under his arm. She'd already kicked off her heels and snuggled into the overstuffed white sofa, another present from Cristo. He'd insisted she take the furniture when he'd sold his apartment and moved back in with his parents. It'd been one of only a few breaks she'd caught in the past six years. The pre-World War II vintage seating her father-in-law had claimed was still good had ceased to be comfortable sometime before she was born.

"So…" Cristo said after pouring the wine and relaxing into the other corner of the sofa.

"He came, we ate, we talked, he kissed me on the cheek. That's all."

Cristo ran a hand through his short, dark hair. "But he's no Matteo."

The sigh escaped. "No."

"You've got to stop comparing every man you meet to him."

"I know, but when you've had prosecco, it's hard to go back to drinking beer."

He leaned forward and took her hand in his. "Don't deify him, Bella. You're a beautiful young woman. You need to let go and love again. Maybe switch to a wine with depth rather than fizz." He released her hand and retreated to the corner again, staring at his glass as he swirled the rich merlot he'd brought during his last visit.

She took a sip of hers. Maybe she did need to move to a different aisle in the man-market. "I'm no good on dates. Never have been. I should just ask your mother to match me with someone. She'll probably have more luck than a computer." Cristo's mother was the epitome of an interfering matron, always suggesting she meet some cousin, friend, distant relation, the green-grocer's godson…

"*Dio* no. Don't you remember the last woman she convinced me to take to dinner?"

They both laughed, the sound bouncing off the walls in the tiny cottage. Bella sipped her wine and stared over the rim at Cristo. He'd been a friend for so long she hadn't seen him as a man. Their gazes locked again and she was the first to look away. *What the hell?*

"She was definitely special," Bella said, forcing aside the moment and trying to get back to their regular camaraderie.

"If your definition of special includes stalking me for three weeks after a single date, then I guess you're right. But you can't be all that socially awkward. You must have dated Matteo."

"Don't you remember? I met Matteo when we crashed into each other. And then he sat beside my hospital bed for three days waiting to get my insurance information."

Cristo laughed again. "That's not the real reason he waited at your bedside. He sent me an email to say he'd met an amazing woman and was going to ask her to marry him before she regained her senses. Next thing I knew I was best man at your wedding."

"He was never one to let the grass grow under his feet." She caught herself using the past tense and sipped her wine to ease the tightening in her throat. "But I knew what I was doing. We had a good marriage."

"It's time, Bella." Cristo had been encouraging her to let go for the past year. She'd filled out the papers to have Matteo legally declared dead but so far hadn't submitted them to the court.

"I know. Even if he is still alive, he obviously doesn't want to be found." There, she managed that without choking up. Baby steps.

Cristo put down his wineglass and stood. "I'd better be going. I have a 4:00 a.m. conference call with the Hong Kong branch."

She followed him to the door. Again the sense of being watched unnerved her. "Cristo, were you at the restaurant tonight, checking I was okay?"

"No, of course not. You're more than capable of looking after yourself. You don't think your date is dangerous, do you?"

"Nah, he was harmless. But make sure you lock the gate behind you."

"Of course." He stared into her eyes and stepped closer. His body heat mingled with his Ralph Lauren aftershave. She inhaled deeply of the manly scent. "Are you worried? Do you want me to stay?"

She forced her eyes from his and searched the yard. But with the moon behind a cloud and no lights beyond those from the cottage, there wasn't much to see.

"No. I'll be fine."

He hesitated a moment longer. She held on to the doorframe and stood on tiptoe to kiss him goodbye on the cheek, as she'd done a thousand times before. Except this time his arm slipped around her waist and unbalanced her. Her hands landed on his chest, and the cheek she'd intended to touch ended up being his lips. His kiss was gentle, nondemanding, a friend asking if they could be more. Before she could figure out a response, he'd already pulled back, setting her on her feet.

"Good night, Bella."

"'Night, Cristo."

He disappeared into the dark within seconds. She glanced again at the yard, but aside from Cristo's feet crunching against the gravel all was quiet. Must just be her nerves overreacting. She bolted the door and then leaned against it.

What had Cristo meant by kissing her? Could he be the one to replace Matteo? She always figured Cristo'd go for a glamorous woman, one able to move among the exalted banking circles he was destined for. Funny how that was the life she'd been planning, before she'd crashed into Matteo. With Kai, who like his father was a cardiothoracic surgeon, her life would have been filled with charity events and opening nights at the opera. Now, much to her parents' disgust, she was a widowed sheep farmer in Sicily.

She poured herself another glass of wine, figuring she'd earned it, and flipped to where she'd stopped reading *The Sheep Farmer's Journal*.

Glamour. That was so ten years ago.

Chapter Two

Matteo took several deep breaths and slid his jaw side to side to give his molars a break from being ground to dust. The doctor had only cleared him to fly provided he get plenty of rest and avoid stress. *As if facing my past isn't the epitome of stress.* Bits and pieces of his memory had returned but not the full picture.

What was clear was that Bella had moved on. First going to dinner with one man then kissing another. It should have made his mission easier: tell her he'd had amnesia then request a divorce. However, he hadn't been prepared for the punch in the heart he'd felt just seeing her again.

Now he had no idea what to do.

His chest was still tight as he saw the taillights of Cristo's SUV disappear down the drive. His best friend. That Lothario had kissed her. His wife! He forced his fists to unclench.

She thought you were dead, his head tried to reason. But his heart wouldn't accept that. At least he'd be able to discover she was still Bella Vanni. For how much longer?

Matteo knocked on the door. His door. His house. His wife. Everything so familiar but so strange.

"Did you forget something, Cristo?" Bella asked as she opened the door. The glass in her hand fell to the floor, shattering on the stone tiles.

"Matteo." His name exhaled from her lips.

"At least you remember me." He tried to keep the anger in his voice, but being so close to her after so many years made the words catch in his throat. Sensations ricocheted through him too fast to identify, scrambling his insides. She was so beautiful. His fingers itched to ease the worry lines around her eyes, caress the furrow between her eyebrows until she smiled. Then the image of her lips on Cristo's returned.

"Matteo," she said again. "You're dead."

"No, I'm very much alive. And you seem to be enjoying yourself. Too bad your game of merry widow is over now."

"Oh my God. I can't believe this."

"Believe it, *bellissima*. I'm home."

"How ... why ... what?" Her whole body began to shake. He took her elbow and steered her toward the sofa in the next room, his shoes crunching on the glass on the floor. His head told him to take things slow, hear her out. His body demanded he pull her into his arms and crush her against him. Hold her until he regained all his memories or this ache in his chest lessened.

She stared at him, her eyes wide, her mouth open. He retreated to the kitchen and got her a glass of water, not sure if he should dash it in her face or give it to her to drink. Returning to where she sat, he let his gaze scan the room, at once familiar and foreign. The recollections he expected never materialized. Had she redecorated? He couldn't remember it with this light, homey feel.

"Where have you been? My God, Matteo. Where have you been for six years?" Her voice was full of anguish. For his disappearance? Or his return?

"In Tunisia mostly. I woke up on the beach with no clothes, no documents, and no memory. It wasn't until I was concussed again earlier this week that I remembered who I am. I raced back to Sicily to find *my wife* ... going to dinner with one man then kissing another in my house."

"I thought you were dead. I waited ... years and years." Pain clouded her eyes, and for one heartbeat he expected the words, "I missed you," to come from her full lips.

"Six years, Matteo. It's been six long, excruciating years without a word from you. So if I want to go out with a hundred men and kiss each and every one then I damn well will. And you will not stroll back into *my* house and tell me different."

He handed her the water and she drank it all at once, her hazel eyes never leaving him. He had to get control of himself or he'd be out on his ass before he could remember if what they'd had was worth fighting for. His body's response to her was off the charts. That had to mean something, didn't it? The pounding in his head amplified.

Kneeling in front of her he searched her face. "I know this is sudden. I'm still adjusting to things myself. But we obviously loved each other once. Don't you think we should see if that's still the case?" He reached for her, but she retreated into the sofa.

17

If he were a clay pot, the heat in her gaze would have shattered him with its sudden intensity. "That's it? 'Hi, honey, I'm home' and you expect to just waltz back in here and pick up where you left off?"

He stumbled to the hard chair next to the fireplace and gripped the armrest just to remain upright. Hadn't they been happy before he left? The pounding of his pulse, his longing to touch her, indicated that he, at least, remembered their passion. Was Bella just in shock at his return? Or was there something more sinister going on? Was she angry because now she'd have to find some other way to get rid of him?

"Are you in love with someone else? Are you in love with Cristoforo?"

"How dare you ask that? You were gone for six years without a word. I thought you were dead."

She hadn't answered his question, and his stomach roiled. "I didn't stay away deliberately. I had amnesia. I didn't even know my own name. Did you think anything less would make me walk out on our life?"

"I don't know. This is such a shock."

He stood and paced the tiny room. What had he expected? For her to just throw herself in his arms and make him promise to never let her go? Instinct screamed, *Hell, yeah*! The reality of the years apart, years when Bella had had to cope on her own without him, knocked him back.

"Where's Papa?" At least he had one uncomplicated relationship.

Her voice softened. "I'm sorry, he's dead. He passed three years ago from pneumonia."

Matteo swallowed the information like a bitter pill.

But he'd partially been prepared for it when he saw that Bella was the registered owner of the farm. Tomorrow he'd grieve for his father. Tonight he needed answers.

"And you've been alone here since then? You've run the farm by yourself?"

"Yes. I hired help when I needed. And I've made some changes so it's not so labor-intensive. It's been tough, but Vanni Farms made a small profit last year."

Amazing. He and his father had barely managed to keep their heads above the poverty line. Bella had accomplished this and more on her own? Incredible. Still, he knew vegetable farming was a lonely business. "Well, you don't have to worry about that anymore. I can look after things now."

Bella stood, the anger in her face intensifying. "I've put my blood, sweat, and tears into this land for the past six years. I'm not just going to stand aside and let you take over. I don't know what you've done, where you've been, or who you've been with. Until I do, until I decide if I want you back, our marriage is on hold. And you keep your mitts off my farm." Her hands were on her hips and her eyes flashed fire.

"This land has been in my family for generations."

"And would now belong to the tax man if I hadn't been here to pay the bills." She took a deep breath. "Matteo, this is too sudden for me. I'm too mixed up. Please, give me the night to think. We can talk in the morning."

"You want me to leave?"

She nodded. "I turned the old barn into a guesthouse. You can stay there tonight."

Tonight, as in tomorrow she'd be over the shock and they could be together again? Or as in tomorrow find someplace else to live? But he could see that arguing with her now would only harm his case. Plus he had his own quagmire of reactions to sort through. So much for explaining his disappearance and then asking for a divorce. Now even the thought of leaving again felt like he was tearing his soul in two. And his body seemed to remember more than his brain. He couldn't bear for her to go to bed with another man's kiss on her lips.

"We both have a lot to think about, Bella. Will you at least let me kiss you hello?"

He stepped into her space and put his hand on her cheek, giving her a moment to pull back if she insisted. As much as he wanted her, he'd never force himself on her. With a sigh, she closed her eyes and leaned in. Maybe he should have started with a kiss and not an accusation. When his lips touched hers, the sigh that escaped came from him. At first he traced the line of her lips with his tongue, savoring the feel of her. She parted them and he slid his tongue inside, tasting the wine she'd had. *Grazie a Dio*, he hadn't remembered how good this was or he'd have gone insane missing her.

Too soon, she broke the contact and took a step back.

"The key to the guesthouse is hanging beside the door. There's a flashlight on the floor next to the fridge. Good night, Matteo."

No "welcome home." No "I remember now how good we were, come into the bedroom." Her cool reception burned in his gut. Patience had never been one of his strong points, but he needed it now.

She folded her arms across her chest and he picked up the key and flashlight. He was barely out the door before he heard the *thunk* of the deadbolt being put in place.

Welcome home, Matteo.

***

Bella pulled off her dress and flung it into the closet. She'd dreamed of Matteo's reappearance for so long, she'd never once thought he'd walk through the door and accuse her of adultery. Damn the man.

Matteo was back. She wanted desperately to believe that they could return to what they had. But life had made her a realist now. She was no longer the sweet, biddable woman anxious to do whatever was needed to keep her man happy. And Matteo was obviously no longer the peasant farmer she'd married.

The hair on the back of her neck stood on end and her scalp tingled. Matteo had definitely changed. There was a hard glint in his eye she'd never seen before. The watch he wore had cost more than her vehicle and she'd seen him take a bag out of some sleek sports car. Were the rumors true?

He'd always had a presence; it had been one of the things that had first attracted her. He never stooped or apologized for who he was. She'd known he would become something one day. Now it appeared he had.

At what price?

There was no way she'd sleep tonight, and the

questions in her head, coupled with the wine she'd drunk, were making her dizzy. Work had kept her sane in the past—it's what she had to concentrate on now. She changed into her jeans and an old T-shirt, pulled her hair up into a ponytail, and grabbed her fleece jacket. There wasn't a lot she could accomplish in the dark, but she'd inspect the fences and note any places that needed repairs.

First, she swept up the broken glass in the kitchen and washed the wine off the tile. Matteo was back. How long would it take to sink in? More importantly, why had he returned?

God, I thought a blind date was the worst thing I'd have to worry about today.

She slipped out the door and went to the shed. She chucked off her running shoes and pulled on her rubber boots, grabbed a large flashlight, and headed out to the paddocks. What would Matteo say when he discovered she'd turned his vegetable farm into a sheep ranch? Or that she'd sold a huge tract of land and bought the access to the beach so the tourists could enjoy a swim in the sea? What if he had no intention of staying? Had he returned to sell the farm and take his share?

Jesus, the endless questions were driving her mad. She should bang on the guesthouse door and demand answers. Except she wasn't prepared to face him again. Not until she could control her body's reaction to his presence. Like that was ever going to happen.

She hauled in two deep breaths of the clean night air and followed the fence line down to the cliff edge, checking each post and the tautness of the wire. She didn't have the physical strength to build a stone fence, the norm in this part of Sicily. Nor had she the money to hire someone to erect it for her. So she'd had to install a cheap timber one, and it was proving true that you get what you pay for. The winds and salt spray from the sea had rotted many of the posts after only two years.

Unfortunately, the task wasn't sufficiently stimulating, especially in the dark, to keep her mind off Matteo. Or his kiss. Especially his kiss. It was still as potent and incredible as she remembered. If she hadn't stopped him when she did, well, she wouldn't be out checking fence posts in the dark, that was damn sure. Her body tingled and infused with heat. Yeah, he'd been a fabulous lover. Maybe they could keep that part of their marriage alive, have some kind of booty call system. Her groan echoed through the night, startling something that scurried in the long grass in front of her.

She was a damn fool. She'd probably step in a hole and break her ankle in the dark. The lapping of the waves against the shore drew her to the beach. Sitting on one of the chairs she left there for the tourists, she watched the moonlight play on the water. For a long time she'd cursed the sea for taking Matteo from her. Now its rhythmic flow and ebb were mesmerizing.

If only the secret of what to do was whispered in the gentle stroke of the water against the sand.

Chapter Three

As soon as a hint of pink lit the eastern sky, Matteo threw back the sheets and dressed. The bed had been surprisingly comfortable, although he hadn't slept much—too many memories now flooding his brain. The whole guesthouse was beautifully appointed. He and Bella had talked about turning the barn into their private house, as living in the cottage with his father had never been a long-term solution. But money had always been an issue. It seemed Bella's fortunes had also turned around in the past six years. How much of it had to do with Cristoforo? He'd always had money.

Matteo's stomach muscles clenched again. He needed answers. His knock on the door was ignored. Trying the handle, he found it unlocked. Perhaps Bella changed her mind in the night. The day was looking up.

But she wasn't in the kitchen or anywhere else in the cottage. He glanced into his father's old room. Bella should have moved in there following Papa's death, as it was the largest bedroom. Although large was a misnomer; the pantry in his place in Tunis was bigger than this. But his father's room sat empty. She still occupied the room he'd shared with her. That had to mean something, right?

Wandering back to the kitchen, he saw a small note propped up against the kettle.

Help yourself to breakfast.

He opened the fridge to find a half liter of milk, a couple of eggs, and some mushrooms. The fridge itself was only slightly cooler than the room. Nothing had been modernized in the cottage. This room he remembered, as it still held the same crappy appliances his father had had since Matteo had been a boy. The guesthouse had all the mod cons. Bella obviously spent any money she had on making more rather than her own comfort.

Even if they didn't stay together, it made no sense for his wife to live like a pauper. He had the money now to make decent renovations. She could move into the guesthouse while they overhauled the main cottage. They could add a few more rooms, create a master suite with floor-to-ceiling windows overlooking the sea, put in a huge soaker tub and a shower big enough for two. His body flooded with heat as the memory resurfaced of sharing the tiny shower with its limited hot water. Bella's naked body pressed against his had cancelled out any discomfort. Maybe they'd keep that. He undid another button on his shirt.

Not that he had plans to stay long on the farm even if they resumed their relationship. He'd finally got the dirt out from under his nails. He was a businessman now, owning luxury resorts and an export business that spanned from Morocco to the Sudan. With no internet and sporadic cell reception, he couldn't run his business here. They'd find a caretaker to manage the land for them. Given Bella's reaction last night, she'd developed quite an affinity for the farm. But surely once she'd seen his other houses, she'd be happy to leave the little cottage behind.

He was getting ahead of himself again. Until he knew what had caused his memory loss and why he'd washed up on a Tunisian beach, he'd keep his plans to himself.

Putting the kettle on the stove to boil, in case he had to settle for tea, he then searched for some way to make coffee. Farrah, an early riser, usually beat him to the office and had it ready. *Dio*, that was another complication in his life. Farrah had been at his side for the past four years, building the export business with him, dealing with the women artisans who didn't trust a foreign man. They worked so well together. But the part of him that had felt shackled by his wedding ring now said he had to give his marriage a fighting chance.

His conscience had a lot to answer for.

The kettle shrieked before he'd discovered some means to distill the few coffee beans he'd found in the door of the freezer.

"Here, let me," Bella said from behind him. She reached around and removed the kettle from the element and took the package of coffee out of his hand. Her long, dark hair was mostly up in a ponytail; however, the wind had teased strands from the elastic until they framed her face like a halo. Her skin was flushed from the cold morning air and she smelled of dirt, salt, and a hint of citrus and lavender. He shoved his hands into his pockets. It seemed his body had no problem remembering what to do with his wife. He wasn't going to be able to do this husband-from-a-distance thing for long.

She bustled about the kitchen, pulling a coffee bean grinder from the back of a cupboard along with a stovetop percolator. The *whizz* as she ground the beans prevented talking. Soon the heady aroma of fresh ground coffee filled the kitchen, and she inhaled deeply.

"I usually just drink instant," she said as she put the grounds into the percolator before adding the water. She put it on the stovetop then turned back to him, her face unreadable. "I was saving the beans for company. I guess you qualify."

"You never used to drink instant coffee. You said it was like dirty water." The comment was out of his mouth before he even properly remembered it. *Merda*, next he'd be declaring his love before he was sure that's what this warm glow signified. Or maybe it was just stress-induced indigestion.

When the brew was ready she poured them each a cup. "Well, I changed. Seemed a waste to make real coffee just for myself."

He let that comment pass. It was too soon to remind her that she wasn't alone anymore.

"Have you been out all night?" There were deep shadows under her eyes and her shoulders slumped.

"Yeah. I needed to check the fencing. See how many new posts I have to order."

She sipped her coffee, staring at him over the rim of her cup as though she couldn't decide if he was real or a figment of her exhausted mind. He felt her confusion in his own chest.

"Sit down, Bella. Let me cook you some breakfast."

Scenes of them cooking together flashed through his brain. Did she remember how they used to feed each other tidbits until there was little left to plate up for the actual meal? It had always been his favorite time of the day, when they chatted and kissed and shared secrets and dreams. Or had the bad eclipsed the good in Bella's mind?

"I can't eat yet. I have to milk the goats first. Coffee will do for now."

"Goats? When did we get goats?"

"*We* didn't get goats. *I* did. Right after the sheep."

"What?"

"This is a sheep farm now. I sold the artichoke fields to Signor Francisco. The mafia has the vegetable market under their control. I couldn't even sell half of the last crop."

"Where'd you get the money to change agriculture?"

"From the bank. I finally put my degree to use, formulated a business plan. Then I got a loan." Her eyes searched his. Did he used to react differently when she mentioned her degree? *Dio*, had he been that much of an ass? He'd proved he could hold his own with all the university graduates he came across in business. It didn't bother him now that she was better educated than him. Her relationship with his friend, however, did.

"Not from Cristoforo?"

"No." She put her half-drunk cup down on the counter. "Milking usually takes me about forty-five minutes. If you have breakfast ready when I get back, I won't say 'no' to an egg and piece of toast. Sorry, I don't have much in the fridge; I wasn't expecting a visitor. Today is market day, and I was planning on going into town this afternoon to get groceries."

"Can I help with the milking? It'll take half the time with the two of us." He'd never milked a goat in his life, but there was no time like the present. Bad day to wear his new handmade loafers, though.

"No, the nannies are very particular and don't like anyone but me touching them. The vet got a nasty bite last time he visited. I assume you'd like to keep all your fingers?"

"That would be preferable. But I'm coming to town with you," he said.

She stared at him for a long moment. "Whatever." Pushing away from the counter she was almost at the door when he stopped her with a hand on her arm.

"Do you have a copy of the business plan for the farm? I'd like to see it." Maybe if he saw her vision for the land he could get his head around the changes. The Vannis had grown vegetables for generations. He couldn't believe his father had let her switch to animals.

"It's in the file cabinet somewhere. Help yourself." She gestured to the little lean-to he'd built next to the house. This time, he closed his eyes on the memories the room evoked. With his father always around, the tiny office had become a place where they could do more than paperwork.

She crossed the yard to a small barn he hadn't noticed before. There was no sway in her hips, and her ponytail didn't bounce from side to side. Bella was buried under such a heavy workload that her depleted lack of enthusiasm and energy was on clear display. He'd spend the next week helping her while figuring out what to do about their relationship.

He found the business plan easily enough in the file cunningly marked "Business Plan & Loan Application." The document was solid and dated almost three years ago, so after his father's death. She hadn't been able to talk the old man around to her way of thinking.

He studied the other papers in the folder. She'd neglected to tell him that while the loan was from the bank, it was guaranteed by Cristoforo Bernini. But according to the ledger on the desk, Bella hadn't missed a payment yet. In fact, the farm was in better shape financially than when he'd left.

He shoved the papers back into the folder and refiled it in the old, battered cabinet. *Dio,* he could remember her excitement when he'd found it in an abandoned building and brought it home. Now he could bring her diamonds and designer dresses. Would she be as happy?

A file marked Legal Documents caught his eye. The first paper was a petition for divorce; under cause Bella had written *Abandonment* all in capitals. His stomach fell to his knees and the coffee he'd drunk threatened to come back up. She thought he'd left her deliberately? No wonder his reception so far had been on the arctic side of cold.

The second document stalled his heart: Petition to have missing person declared dead. The only thing needed was her signature.

Bella had given up and was ready to move on. Was he too late to save his marriage?

***

Bella tucked a strand of hair behind her ear as she dragged herself back to the cottage. Although she was physically exhausted, an electrical energy zapped through her veins. Didn't take a psychologist to know it was anticipation at seeing Matteo. He'd always had this effect on her. Even after two years of marriage it hadn't lessened. But was spectacular sex enough to base a marriage on? Probably not. She needed more now.

Her steps slowed as she approached the front door, acutely aware that she smelled of goat and sweat and had coffee breath. She'd done little actual work on the farm during the two years before Matteo had disappeared. Her role had been to look after the paperwork, housework, and clean for a few of the old bachelor neighbors to bring in some extra money. Matteo and his father had held the opinion that a woman's job was in the home, not digging in the dirt or fixing the rundown tractor. Well, she'd showed them. Even her father-in-law had admitted before he died that she'd made a damn good farmer.

Still, it would be nice to have a shower before she ate.

Before she could grab the door handle, Matteo opened it. "I've run a bath for you in the guesthouse. You look exhausted. Can you make it, or shall I carry you?"

Temptation, thy name is Matteo. "I can walk."

He put his arm around her shoulders, and she forced herself not to lean against him. She had to stay strong, not let herself rely on him again. Who knew if he would stay? If he left, it would be crueler than before, because this time it would be a conscious decision.

Provided it was true what he said about the amnesia.

"If you give me a list, I can get what you need in town. You're too tired to go shopping," he said as he opened the door to the steam-filled bathroom. A delicate scent of lavender and lemons tickled her nose. The bath salts were her latest business venture, but so far only her guests had used them.

Damn. Guests.

"I have to go. I use the wifi at the café to check online bookings for this place. Oh, God, I have people coming to stay here tomorrow." It had been all ready for them. Now she'd need to wash the sheets and remake the bed, clean whatever mess Matteo had made, restock the bath salts… She mentally added the things to her to-do list and groaned. Sleep would have to wait for another day.

"I'll move my things into my father's old room while you have a bath. Then I'll get this place sorted. Do you have extra sheets?"

She should protest his assumption that he could just move into the cottage. But as his name was still on the deed, there wasn't a lot legally she could do to turf him out. "Yeah, in the linen cupboard in the upstairs hall. You know how to change a bed?" He and his father had lived like two bachelors before their marriage, rarely changing the bedding.

"I worked at a resort for six months doing everything from cleaning the rooms to tending bar. I can make a bed." Matteo lingered, his eyes searching hers. He lifted a hand and tucked another strand of her hair behind her ear. "Relax for a few minutes, *bellissima*. We have a lot to talk about when you're ready."

They did. They were married strangers. The past and present were colliding, creating a vortex ready to suck in her lonely heart.

He closed the door behind him and she let the tears fall. Would he bring her back to life? Or destroy her once and for all time?

Chapter Four

Matteo stripped the sheets from the bed and tried not to think of the many times he'd done it before. His first year of memory loss had been hard. He'd worked every job he could get, sometimes for just pennies an hour, trying to earn enough money to investigate his past. But because the Arab Spring had been sweeping through Tunisia, the government had been in complete disarray and didn't care about a lone man unable to prove who he was.

Why hadn't Bella reported him missing? That was the question that gnawed hardest at his soul.

He pulled out the replacement linen and quickly remade the bed, packed up his toiletries, and took the used sheets and his bag to the main cottage. He lingered for a moment in front of Bella's room. The room they'd shared as husband and wife. Would they share it again? Or had too much time elapsed for them to go back? He was definitely different from the poor vegetable farmer she'd married. He could only assume that she'd changed as well. He had to get to know his own wife all over again.

He threw his bag into his father's old room, shutting down the grief until he had time to deal with it, and went back to the guesthouse, wanting to have the meager breakfast ready by the time Bella came out of the tub. *Dio*, how he'd have liked to join her in the scented water. Run his hands over her smooth skin, taste the promise of ecstasy on her lips. He grew hard and forced his mind to cooking. Feed her first. She looked thin enough to blow away with the next gust of wind.

A delicate scent of lavender and lemons flowed over him, and he turned. Bella stood in the doorway, her dark hair now falling in soft waves around her shoulders and down her back. She wore the short satin robe he'd pulled from her closet, her nipples hard and clearly showing through the fabric. He swallowed; his blood pressure went through the roof.

"I made a mushroom omelet as there were only three eggs. And there's no more coffee. Would you like tea?" *Merda*, he sounded like the waiter he'd also been years ago.

"Tea would be great." She sat at the table, and when she crossed her legs the robe parted to reveal her strong, lean thighs. He poured himself a glass of water and drank it all at once.

He placed the plate with the toast and eggs in front of her and made the tea. "Where's yours?" she asked as she hesitated with a forkful of omelet by her lips.

"There wasn't enough for both of us. I'll eat when we go into town."

"Oh for God's sake, Matteo, there's no need to play the martyr. There's plenty. Grab a fork and help yourself." She pushed the plate equidistance between them and waited until he picked up a utensil. He was ravenous, having skipped dinner last night as he'd waited in the car for her to finish her date.

His stomach roiled, and he put his fork down after one bite. This was the first issue they had to tackle. Although he wasn't sure if he was ready to hear her answer.

He reached across and took her free hand in his, running his thumb over the calluses on her palm. It was hard to keep his focus. The memories tumbled through him, leaving a path of destruction in their wake—the passion, the love, the tenderness.

He'd had rough hands like hers when they first married. And she'd often commented on how much she loved his strong fingers on her body. Now his were smooth and soft and hers were rough. His heart squeezed painfully in his chest. His delicate wife reduced to a farm worker because life had stolen six years from them. He had to make it up to her.

Matteo cleared his throat of emotion. "Bella—"

The crunch of gravel outside had both of them glancing out the window. "It's Cristo," she said. Before he could reply, she abandoned her breakfast and went to the door, throwing it open, never mind the fact she was barely dressed.

He was about to find out just how close the relationship between his wife and former buddy really was.

**

"Cristo, in here," she called out as her friend exited his vehicle and started toward the cottage.

"Bella, I got your text, but I don't understand. What do you mean Matteo's back?" His gaze swept her just as a breeze plastered the fabric to her body, leaving nothing to the imagination. She hadn't wanted to put her dirty clothes back on after her bath, and the only thing Matteo had left in the bathroom was her old robe, his first-year anniversary present to her. When she dared look at Cristo's face, he had the same expression Matteo had worn when he'd seen her in the doorway ten minutes ago.

Lust.

Guess I'm not as old and hag-like as I thought. Before she could answer Cristo's question, however, Matteo came up behind her. His arms snaked around her waist, and he pulled her back against his hard body. His breath caressed her neck, its warmth slithering down her cleavage. He'd done it a million times during their marriage, but why did it feel so possessive now? Had he seen the look in Cristo's eyes as well?

"Cristoforo." Her husband's deep voice vibrated through her, and his arm tightened against her abdomen. She pulled away, not ready to play this game now.

"Matteo. What the hell?" Cristo was as stunned as she'd been last night.

"Yes, hell would be a good way to describe it. I'm back now. To claim my wife."

"I'm not an object, Matteo." She crossed her arms over her chest until she saw both men staring pointedly at her breasts, the fabric pressed tight against them. "Oh for God's sake," she muttered under her breath. They were behaving like teenagers. You'd think they'd never seen a set of boobs before.

"Bella's right. You were gone a long time. She's not a toy that you can just toss aside and come back for when it suits you. She's a strong, beautiful woman who deserves a man who treasures her, not abandons her the moment things get tough."

She stared at Cristo. Uh, what was going on here?

"I didn't abandon Bella. I had an accident and lost my memory. The fact remains, she's *my* wife." This time Matteo crossed his arms, his biceps bulging under his T-shirt. She shoved down the shiver of awareness. This was not helping. She needed to make rational decisions, not be turned on by his body.

"Bella?" Cristo ignored Matteo's aggressive stance and turned to her. "Do you want Matteo back? Because you have options."

Okay, those must have been magic mushrooms in the omelet because she was hallucinating. After six years alone, she now had two men to choose from?

"Options?"

Cristoforo strode over and took her hand in his. "I've wanted you for years, Bella. I've waited for you to be ready to love again. I know Matteo once held your heart, but you've changed. He's obviously changed. You can still file for divorce. Choose a man who will stay with you…"

A deep growl came from Matteo. "I did not leave willingly. I still don't know what happened. That part of my memory hasn't returned. But I will find out. And when I do—"

She followed the line of Matteo's gaze and saw a blue SUV lumbering over the pothole-riddled drive.

Had her guests come a day early? She could read the Trip Advisor comment now: *Arrived to find hostess practically naked with two men fighting over her. Visit went downhill from there.*

But she was expecting a family with two young children. Instead, a tall, blond-haired man got out, his eyes hidden behind sunglasses. It couldn't be…

"Kai!" she said. Cristo dropped her hand. "I didn't think you were coming. Your text said you'd had a change of plans."

"Hello, Pop-Tart. I changed them back. Couldn't bear to not see you again."

Her laugh came out strangled and too high-pitched. She was on the edge of losing it. Men *were* like buses. You wait and wait and wait, and then three come along at once.

Kai strolled over, ignoring the other two men, and hugged her, swinging her off her feet. "You in a bit of trouble?" he whispered in her ear.

"Not yet. But things are definitely getting interesting."

He put her back on her feet but kept his arm around her shoulders—protective, big brother style.

"Who's this?" Matteo looked like he might explode.

"Kai Andersen, my ex-fiancé. Kai, let me introduce you to Matteo, my estranged husband, and Cristoforo, a good friend who now claims to want me."

"Is this a meeting to see who gets to have you? Because if so, I'm in."

"What?" she, Matteo, and Cristo all asked at once.

"Sure," Kai added, gazing down at her, his face

full of mischief. "We were engaged once, why not actually get married? How are we doing this? Arm wrestle? Rock, paper, scissors? Or should we just drop our pants, show our dicks, and see who has the biggest?"

She was tempted just to walk away and let them fight it out between them. Then she could decide if the victor was worthy of her. But there was too much at stake to let three testosterone-fueled men duke it out in front of the guesthouse. Matteo looked like he was about to kill.

A shiver raced down her spine. She'd never thought he was capable of violence until this moment.

"A date," she blurted out. "You each get one date with me to convince me you're my ideal husband."

"May I remind everyone that Bella already has a husband," Matteo said. "Me."

Cristo and Kai ignored him. "So," Cristo asked her, "who goes first?"

"Seems only fair we should do this alphabetically … by last name. Kai, you can take me out tomorrow night, if you're still here."

"I'll be here," he replied. "I wouldn't miss this for anything."

"Then Cristo gets Saturday and Matteo on Sunday. I can't believe I'm saying this, but I'll decide on Monday—not who I'll marry, or continue to be married to," she added quickly, "but who I'll keep dating to see if it works out."

Kai nodded happily, Cristo accepted with magnanimity, and Matteo looked like he'd rather have his fingernails pulled off with pliers.

"Now, if you gentlemen will excuse me, I'll go get dressed before any more men show up and my whole week gets filled." She turned on her heel and strode toward the cottage.

Good God, it wasn't even 9:00 a.m. yet.

Chapter Five

Matteo's teeth were still clenched three hours later as he drove into town with Bella. What the hell? He had to compete for his wife in a date-off? Her knees bounced up and down and she wrung her hands in her lap. She'd lingered in completing the morning chores, and then she'd argued with him for ten minutes about whose car to take. He'd insisted they travel in luxury.

She deserved luxury. In addition to the sheep and goats, she also had a camel—a camel!—a horse, a donkey, two dogs, at least three cats that he'd seen, four beehives, and a couple of rabbits. And from the activity of the rabbits, there would be more of them before long.

"Why do you have a camel?" he asked. Their relationship was too explosive a topic at the moment. He'd stick with the mundane.

"I kind of inherited him. Some guy asked if I would stable his camel for a few months. He paid me for the first two, and then disappeared."

"And you kept it?"

"What else was I supposed to do? Besides, Akbar pays his way. I take him to some of the local festivals and charge ten euros a ride." She shrugged as if camel ownership was commonplace.

"And the rest of the menagerie—I assume most of those came after my father died?"

"Yeah. I guess I'm a soft touch. People have animals they can't care for anymore and I take them. But they all come in handy. The children who stay at the guesthouse love that I have a petting zoo on the premises."

"Do many tourists come to stay?" He'd never thought of the farm as a holiday destination. To him, it represented endless work and hard times.

"I'm booked all summer and the first month of the fall. By the end of the year, the guesthouse will have paid for its renovation, and then next year will be all profit."

He could see the pride in her face. This was the Bella he needed to understand.

He parked the Maserati near the village square so all who'd known him since he was a child could see he'd returned a successful man. Plus, he'd be better able to keep his eye on it as they picked up the things on Bella's list.

Lacing his fingers through hers, they made their way toward the district agricultural office. As they turned the corner, his high school math teacher, Signor Fossi, was walking toward them. All the color drained from the older man's face, his eyes widened, and his mouth dropped open. Matteo's smile faded as horror replaced shock on the teacher's face. Was there something terrible behind him? He was about to turn around when the teacher crossed the road and hurried his steps to scoot around the corner and out of sight within seconds. Odd. He'd had a good relationship with his teachers. He hadn't been the most popular kid; there had been too much work to do on the farm for him to indulge in after-school activities. Still, he'd been well liked, hadn't he? Was his mind playing tricks on him—giving him false memories?

Several other people passed them before they reached the sanctuary of the agricultural office. Some faces he knew, others were a blank, but their reaction to him was all the same. Disgust. By the time he pushed open the door of the building that had almost been a second home to him, his chest was heavy; it hurt to draw a deep breath, and Bella's hand was so tight in his he wouldn't be surprised if his fingers were white from lack of blood.

He pretended to read the paper while she reported her monthly production totals. He couldn't stomach going to the counter with her and facing more adverse reactions. What was with the people in the village?

Dio, he hadn't expected a parade, but a few hugs and some exclamations of happiness wouldn't have gone amiss. Many of these people had known him since he was a baby. Surely they would be pleased to see he'd returned at last.

As they exited the building, Bella took his hand in hers and walked beside him with her head high. "Just ignore them," she whispered as the butcher's wife spat on the road in front of him before crossing herself.

Bella ordered some new fence posts and feed for the animals and arranged for a load of gravel to even out the driveway. The people she dealt with stared at him openly, but not one asked him a single question or welcomed him back. Thankfully, her bits of business were done quickly.

"What's going on, Bella?" he asked as a mother hurried her three children along while watching him out of the corner of her eye.

"I'll tell you later. I'm starving. Let's get some lunch at the café." She pulled him into a glass-fronted shop that had been a florist six years ago. The village hadn't changed. A few stores were different but the general air of a small, centuries-old market town, well past its age of glory, was the same. People still dressed up, as though shopping were an important affair worthy of their best outfit. In his custom-made suit and handcrafted shoes, he should fit in. Yet he didn't.

The cobblestone streets and narrow, twisty alleys he'd walked so many times no longer wanted him here.

A woman in her mid-twenties came around the counter, gave Bella a big hug, and then raked him with her gaze. "Who's this?"

"This is Matteo, my husband." At least Bella had dropped the "estranged" bit when introducing him this time.

"The one who disappeared?"

"The same. I don't have a whole stack of them hidden around the world. Matteo, this is Angela. She's an American like me, married a Sicilian. And she makes the best cappuccino on the island."

"You're just saying that because I let you use my computer." Angela retreated behind the counter and returned with a battered laptop.

"Bella doesn't lie," Matteo said. Again, the words fell from his mouth without thought. Did he truly believe them? Or was it what he wanted to believe? He did know that for the first time since his return, his wife looked relaxed and happy, carefree. "Can we have two cappuccinos, and I'll have a large serving of whatever that fabulous smell is."

"Homemade minestrone soup."

Bella nodded. "I'll have a bowl, too."

"Coming right up." Angela's American accent was much more pronounced than Bella's. In fact, Bella had spoken perfect Italian during her business discussions. She'd barely managed a word of his native language when they'd first married.

How would she take to learning Arabic?

"Excuse me, but I need to do a bit of work," Bella said as she powered up the laptop. "I come here three times a week and borrow Angela's computer to check on bookings for the guesthouse and orders for the various other products I sell."

"No problem. I need to make a couple of calls as well."

Angela put the coffees on the table in front of them, her gaze rarely leaving his face. At least there wasn't the disgust and fear he'd seen in the eyes of the other villagers.

Bella's complete concentration was on the screen, a small smile on her lips. He pulled out his cell phone and called Farrah; he'd been trying to arrange a sales meeting with an American department store, but so far hadn't been successful.

Farrah answered the phone on the fourth ring, and he could picture her staring at the screen a moment then squaring her shoulders before flicking the icon to accept. He'd watched her do this numerous times when she was about to take a call she didn't particularly want to answer. It would be the first time he'd be the one on the other side of the unwanted phone call.

"Mario, how are you?" The chill in her voice reached across the three hundred kilometers between them and frosted his eyelashes.

"I'm good. And you?" His gaze shot to Bella, but her complete concentration was on the screen in front of her. His plan to ask for a divorce so he could start a relationship with Farrah stuck in his throat.

"Fine." It could have been the poor cellular service, but there seemed to be a hitch in Farrah's voice. And it didn't matter what language they spoke, "fine" from a woman's mouth never meant that. However, sitting across from his wife didn't seem an appropriate time to question another woman's real state of heart.

"Have we heard back from Saks?" he asked.

The pause on the other end was long. "No. I sent them another message yesterday."

"And the shipment to Lafayette in Paris?" This conversation couldn't be more painful if each syllable were a razor blade slicing into his skin. Normally, he could barely get a word in edgewise with Farrah. She was enthusiasm personified when it came to their business.

"It eventually made it. About a tenth of the items were damaged, but the rest were okay. I've arranged to ship some pieces from storage to complete the contract."

"Excellent. Anything else I need to know?"

"No. I've got it all covered." Another long pause and an audible indrawn breath. "Do you know when you'll be back?"

It was his turn to hesitate. "Things here are a bit more complicated than I expected."

Had she hung up? Her voice was strained when finally she said, "I miss you. The office isn't the same without you here."

He shut his eyes, picturing Farrah's face. "I'll talk to you soon." He cancelled the call before either of them said something they'd regret.

When he looked up, Bella was staring at him and not the computer.

"You speak Arabic."

"Yes, I had a crash course waking up in a country where it was the main language."

"And who's the woman?"

Was Bella jealous? Her eyes were slightly narrowed and her lips a thin line. "Farrah Meddeb. I hope you'll meet her soon."

"She's coming here?"

Angela arrived at that moment with the soup, and Bella moved the computer out of the way. He caught a brief glimpse of a website for Vanni Farms and made a mental note to look at it later.

"I'm hoping you'll come to Tunisia with me."

"Are you kidding me? It may have escaped your notice, but I run a farm, with animals that expect to be fed every day. I can't just leave anytime I want."

"And I run multimillion-dollar businesses throughout North Africa. I can't do that from a farmhouse kitchen."

She tilted her head to the side. "What kind of businesses?"

"I have six luxury resorts in North Africa. Two in Tunisia and one each in Egypt, Libya, Algeria, and Morocco. I'm in negotiations to buy additional hotels in India and Myanmar."

"And what does this Farrah do? Is she your assistant?"

"No. She's my business partner in another venture, an artisans' cooperative."

Bella took a spoonful of soup and didn't meet his eyes. "Seems like we're right back to where we were before you barged back into my life. I can't leave Sicily and you won't live here. Unless you're about to suggest some kind of weekend marriage where we alternate visiting each other?"

"I don't remember everything about our marriage, Bella. But the bits I do lead me to believe that neither of us would be happy with that arrangement."

Color tinged her cheeks. "No. Probably not."

A couple entered the café, looked at him, and walked back out. His smile wavered. Those were two of his old schoolmates, Enrico and Paola. They'd often swapped lunches to give each other a bit of variety. Something was definitely wrong in this town. A sickening feeling spread through him, and it was all he could do to finish his soup despite how delicious it was.

Was it because they'd thought him dead and now he'd returned hale and hearty? Folklore and superstition had always been the backbone of life in rural Sicily, but it was hard to imagine that people of his generation were ensnared by such fears. Maybe they thought he'd been to prison and was newly released. Whatever the cause, he was clearly *persona non grata*. Unless it was Bella who prompted such ostracism. But what could she have done?

"I think we'll get the groceries at the store rather than the market," Bella said. "I need to get back to the farm, and it will be quicker."

"Okay."

She said a fond farewell to Angela, who waved away all his attempts to pay her for the lunch. "Just be good to her," Angela said, her eyes wary.

When they got to the grocery store Bella raced around like she was on some game show where she had to fill her cart in the least amount of time to win the prize. In the checkout line, she ignored the stares and whispers of the other customers. Had Bella been dealing with this hostility for the past six years? He wanted to shout at everyone to give her a break. She was contributing to the economy and bringing paying tourists to the area. But the way she tightened her hand on his when he opened his mouth gave him second thoughts.

When the village was in the rearview mirror, she sank into the seat as though exhausted and rubbed her bare ring finger on her left hand with her thumb.

"What the hell is wrong with everyone? Have they acted that way toward you all this time?" He forced his hands to relax on the wheel.

"At first, when you disappeared. But it got better after a while and people forgot. Most of the villagers are pretty friendly to me now. At least they were."

Then it must be him. "I don't understand. What did people have to forget?"

She stared at him for another moment before rubbing her finger again. "Matteo, do you really not remember what happened the day you left?"

He slowed the car and glanced over. Her face was pale. "No. Nothing. I remember celebrating an anniversary—our second?—and then waking up in the hospital in Tunis."

"Can you pull over?"

He parked the Maserati at a viewpoint up the road. Before he could ask what the problem was, she got out of the car and stood staring at the view, her arms wrapped around herself. He joined her but kept his distance, although every cell in his body screamed at him to hold her.

"Tell me." The renewed fear in her eyes ate at him like a rat gnawing on a bone.

She sucked in a huge breath and continued staring at the sea. The *scirocco*, the hot wind from Africa, blew her hair in long strands behind her. "You weren't the only one to go missing that day. Three others, men you knew, also disappeared. Five days later, their bodies washed up on shore. The boat was found two weeks after that, bobbing in the middle of the Med, covered in blood. It was assumed that you had also died. And it was all my fault."

A tear glistened on her cheek, and he couldn't resist. He pulled her against his chest. The relief that swept through him to have her in his arms again was palpable. "How could it be your fault?" He was still trying to assimilate the rest of the information, but her guilt had to stop now.

"The farm was going through a particularly rough patch. The roof had blown off the barn and the tractor needed major repairs. We were living on artichokes and bell peppers. I casually remarked that it would be nice to have a bit of fish once in a while, as we lived right next to the sea. So while I was at my cleaning job, you went down to the docks and hopped on a boat with three of your old schoolmates. If I hadn't asked for fish … if I'd have kept my mouth shut and been happy with what we had…"

His chest tightened. How long had she tormented herself with these thoughts? "Bella, it wasn't your fault. I went fishing. I was probably sick of vegetables as well. There's no way you could have known what was to happen."

"That's what your father said." At least his dad hadn't laid on the guilt. He had a vague recollection that his wife and father had had a tenuous relationship. After his mother's betrayal, Papa never believed Bella would stick around and had done everything possible to talk Matteo out of the marriage.

"What's with the people in town?"

"The men who washed up on the beach—Stefano, Ciro, and Leonardo—they were known *Mafiosi*, and according to the newspaper reports they'd all been shot in the head. The boat's deck had everyone's blood but yours. There was talk, even then, that you had been the gunman and your body hadn't washed up on the beach with the others because you'd taken off in another vessel. Now you're back and clearly wealthy. The rumors have started again, and people think you are an assassin. I've just got Vanni Farms profitable. No one will buy from me if they think you're a killer."

He swallowed, wracking his brain for any memory of the day he'd left. Nothing. Maybe later he'd go down to the docks to see if something triggered a flashback. His chest tightened and he could see the apprehension in Bella's face. "Do you think I killed those men?"

She hesitated. *Merda*, she thought he was a murderer?

"I don't believe the man I married, the man I loved, could kill in cold blood. But I can see what others might think. Everyone knew we were destitute. It's not beyond imagining that a man in your position would take the contract, lay low for a few years, and then return to claim what was once his."

"I ... I can't imagine killing anyone, even less three people, three friends, in cold blood. No matter how desperate I was. I'm innocent, Bella." Her name came out all broken. Damn his voice for failing him now.

Dio, he hoped his instinct was right. What if he had done it?

He stared into her eyes and saw the apprehension. A shiver bumped down his spine.

"Is that why you didn't report me missing?"

***

The rawness of Matteo's voice grated her heart.

"What do you mean? Of course I reported you missing, before midnight on the day you disappeared."

Bella searched his face. The hurt in his eyes was unmistakable. He thought she hadn't loved him? Then why had he returned when he remembered who he was?

"Really? Because, as soon as I was released from hospital, I went to the Italian embassy. But they said no one matching my description was on their missing persons list. They even showed me the files." His arms that had been holding her tight now fell to his side.

"I don't know what happened then. I went down to the police station and filed the report that night. I called everyone I even thought you might know. Your dad drove around the island for days, checking every cove, every bay, to see if you'd managed to make it back to shore. Cristo came from England to search..." She reached out to touch his face. His jaw was smooth; in a few hours it would be stubbly again. Matteo was six foot two of muscled Sicilian man, but at this moment all she saw was the uncertainty in his eyes.

"So you had nothing to do with my accident?"

It took a moment to absorb the impact of his words. The hand that had been caressing his jaw flew to her mouth.

"How could you even think that? You were my husband. I loved you. I searched for you, prayed for you to return, cried when each wedding anniversary passed and you were still gone. When everyone else told me to give up and have you declared dead, I wouldn't do it."

He reached for her again and she resisted. But the lure of being held by him, if only for a moment, to absorb some of his strength, was too much to resist.

"I am still your husband, Bella," he said, his lips rubbing against her temple as he spoke.

Even though it was the last thing she wanted to do, she stepped away from him. "But I'm not your wife. Not in the way I was. I'm a different person now. Stronger in some ways, but I also know my weaknesses. I can't afford another six years of getting over you. We need to step back and…"

"And what?"

She turned toward the sea, the breeze tangling her hair. Unfortunately, Bob Dylan wasn't right, the answer wasn't blowing in the wind.

"I don't know," she said past the lump in her throat. "I just know I need some time to sort it all out in my head. We need to know what really happened the day you disappeared before we can truly move on."

"What if we never find out? The doctor said amnesia is unpredictable. I may regain all my memories, or I may always have a blank space of days that will never be filled. I don't remember the state of our marriage just before my accident. When I hold you though, I remember the amazing feel of being inside you, of never wanting to leave. I remember the calm that would wash over me when you took my hand in yours. I remember the happiness that flowed from my every pore when you smiled at me. But I also have this sensation… I don't know if it's a memory trying to resurface or just a personal hang-up, but there was something wrong, a reason we weren't truly content."

"It was poverty. We were stone broke. You and your father were too proud to ask for help. The farm was going under and we were all stressed. I'd started to wonder if you'd married me hoping I'd bring money to our marriage. But when my parents disowned me, all I came to you with was my heart. It didn't seem like enough."

"Your love is all I've ever wanted, Bella."

"Was it? You can't say that because you don't remember. Why did you come back, Matteo? You seem to have a great life in Tunisia, two thriving businesses. Why not just stay missing?"

It was his turn to stare at the sea. "Because I needed to know what I'd lost before I could move on with my life."

"And now that you know?"

"I'm even more confused than before."

Amen to that.

Chapter Six

Bella rushed into the cottage and barreled straight into Matteo's chest. Everywhere she went, he was there, filling the space, sucking the oxygen from her lungs, making her body vibrate. How was she supposed to be calm and serene when he unsettled her with every look?

"You can't really mean to do this," he said as she forced herself to walk away. "You already have a husband."

"I'm going out with Kai. We've known each other since childhood. I'll be safe with him."

Her guests had arrived late, but thankfully they were repeat visitors so it only took a couple of minutes to show them around and remind them how to get to the beach. But she was still rushed to get ready for her "date."

"I saw the way he looked at you. He wants you," Matteo said.

"Wants me back, you mean. If you recall, I was engaged to him before I married you."

Matteo's eyes darkened. It wasn't fair to push his buttons, but she wanted him as off-balance as she was feeling.

With the constant tension that swirled between her and Matteo, she was looking forward to an evening with an old friend. Their breakup had been amicable. They'd gotten engaged because they'd been young and thought the friendship between them was love. It wasn't until she'd met Matteo that she knew that real love was holding someone's hand and believing that, despite the fact blight had destroyed half the crop, it would still be profitable, even though you couldn't see how. She and Kai had kept in touch over the years, sharing the pain of each other's tragedies. Now they were both on the mend, emotionally. Or she had been, until Matteo showed up.

Kai couldn't be serious about wanting to get back together with her, could he?

She raced into the shower, ignoring the scowl on Matteo's face. He was a fine one to judge her for going out with another man when he spoke like a lover to Farrah on the phone. Although she couldn't understand their conversations in Arabic, she recognized that soft voice he'd used. It was the same way he used to speak to her.

She normally took quick showers—to save on the water heating and because they reminded her of some of the most intimate moments with Matteo—but she might have actually set a record with this one. At least she didn't smell like goat anymore.

"Where's he taking you?" Matteo asked as she dashed between the bathroom and her bedroom with only a towel wrapped around her. His eyes flared as he took in her bare legs. An answering heat flooded through her. *Why am I going out with Kai again? Oh yeah, to get some space from Matteo to think rationally about what I want from life.*

"Probably just to the restaurant in his hotel in Agrigento. You're not planning on following us, are you?"

He hesitated so long she thought he wasn't going to answer so he didn't lie. "No. I won't follow. I trust you, Bella."

Was that some kind of snide insinuation that she didn't trust him? Swallowing down the quick retort that would only launch an argument, she shut the door in his face instead. She didn't have time for these head games now. She hadn't even decided what to wear when she heard Kai's rental SUV make its way up the newly smoothed driveway. Matteo had insisted on paying for the gravel and the guy to spread and flatten it. She'd protested to maintain her independence, but secretly she was relieved. It had to be done but was going to take a big chunk out of her already meager operating budget.

She peeked through the bedroom window. Seeing what Kai was wearing would give her some idea about how fancy to dress. Matteo was at his side before Kai had even shut his driver's door. The two men were in earnest discussion, although thankfully no fists were flying. Yet.

Kai wore a suit but no tie. Semiformal then. Grabbing the first dress her hand came to, she tugged it on, fluffed up her hair and went out to her husband and her date. God, this was screwed up.

"Hey, Pop-Tart you ready to go?" Kai asked as she stood in the cottage doorway. His use of her annoying but oddly adorable nickname spurred her forward. Kai was fun. She was ready for fun.

"Pop-Tart?" Matteo asked, his possessive gaze sweeping over her. She resisted the urge to put a hand on her cleavage.

"Bella was always popping up every time I turned around as a kid. And she was so sweet, it seemed the perfect name for her," Kai explained.

She'd popped up on him continually because she'd had a crush on him since she was seven and he eleven, when their parents had become best friends. Kai was fun, easygoing, familiar. Warmth spread through her when she saw him. Matteo, on the other hand, was intense, driven, and she was beginning to feel that she hardly knew him at all. But when their eyes met, the heat that seared her insides wiped all thought of Kai from her mind. She'd been claimed. But her husband didn't need to know that.

"I'm ready. Bye, Matteo."

Kai opened the passenger door for her, waiting until she'd settled herself before closing it. He shook hands with Matteo, much to her husband's surprise, before climbing behind the wheel.

"If another man were driving away with my wife, I'd look just like him," Kai said, nodding at Matteo through the windshield.

"I need some space to think. And you don't really want me back, do you, Kai?"

He turned the vehicle around and waited until they were past the gate before answering. "I want you to be happy." He left it at that and the rest of the drive they spoke of acquaintances and his family.

As expected, he took her to the restaurant attached to his hotel. "Have you spoken with your parents?" Kai asked after the waiter took their drinks order. He should have postponed his question until after she had a martini in hand.

"No. We're not speaking."

"I could talk to your mom. She didn't look very happy the last time I saw her. I'm sure it's because she misses you."

"No. It's not up for discussion, Kai. They made it clear I had to choose between them and Matteo. When I picked him, they disowned me."

"That was years ago. People mellow."

"Not them. When Matteo first went missing, I swallowed my pride and begged them to lend me money to pay for a proper search for him. They said, and I quote, 'If your husband has left you already, we're not wasting our good money to track down someone we never wanted you to marry in the first place. You made your choice, now live with it.'"

Kai placed a hand over hers on the table. It was warm and strong. "You should have come to me. I'd have given you the cash."

"You were working for Doctors Without Borders. Besides, it seemed wrong to ask my ex-fiancé to fund a search for the man I left him for."

He smiled at that. "I never resented you for breaking off our engagement. It gave me an excuse to do what I wanted with my life rather than what my parents wanted. I pretended I was heartbroken and went off to Africa, where I met my beautiful Tsion. So I thank you for that." A shadow of grief clouded Kai's eyes. His wife had tragically been killed last year.

Bella swallowed past the lump in her throat. "But now you're back in the States doing what they wanted from the first." Should she go back to America as well, do what her parents wanted? Marry a man with money and social ranking. Do lunches and attend charity events. She shuddered at the thought.

"And you can bet they remind me of that all the time. If it were just me, I'd still be working in Africa. But the United States is the best place for Joy. You're going to laugh: I've even moved back in with my parents so they can look after their granddaughter if I get called to the hospital in the middle of the night."

She did laugh. What was it with her and men who lived with their parents? "I was hoping you'd bring your daughter with you. I'd love to meet her."

"Maybe next time. My mother was organizing some fundraising party and couldn't come with me, so there was no one to look after Joy while I was in meetings."

The waiter placed their drinks in front of them and then asked for their dinner order. Bella took a sip of her martini, the alcohol warming a path down her throat.

She stared at Kai over the rim of her glass. They'd always be friends, but it could never be more. There was no longer a spark of attraction between them. Plus, he was so entrenched in his high-society life, she just couldn't see herself as the plus one at all his charity events. "At least your parents came around. Did they ever accept your wife?"

"Yeah, the day I told them they were going to be grandparents. You should try that."

"I don't think Matteo and I are about to have a baby."

"You wanted him back for years. What's the problem?"

"He's changed. He's not the uncomplicated man I wed. Before, if you'd taken me out to dinner, he'd have kissed me and told me to have a great time. Now, he's jealous and keeps telling me I'm a married woman and shouldn't be going out with another man."

"Before he was sure of your love. Now he's not. Uncertainty is not a pleasant state for a man. It makes us irrational."

"It's not only that. He's got money and speaks Arabic and runs some sort of artisan cooperative as well as a bunch of resort properties. I don't know him anymore. The Matteo I knew loved the land and had never wanted to leave it. The one in my kitchen now sounds like he can't wait to put it behind him. And there's still the whole mystery about his disappearance."

"What are you going to do?"

"I don't know. I was hoping you'd have some advice."

"Come back to New York, marry me, help me raise my daughter, and we'll grow old together as best friends."

Kai sat back as the waiter arrived with their appetizers. Bella glanced at the server's face. Thank God, he didn't take any interest in Kai's weird proposal.

"Kai, are you serious?" she asked as the waiter retreated.

"Yes. I don't want Joy to grow up without a mother. But I'll never love again, at least not the way I loved Tsion. I can't go through that a second time." He put his hand over hers, glaring at the waiter as he approached with a pepper grinder. "We've been friends for years, Bella. We could have a good life together. It won't be the grand passions of our first marriages, but do you really want to go through that heartbreak again if it doesn't work out with Matteo?"

"I don't know what to say." He had a point. She was terrified of letting Matteo back into her life, not sure she could cope with a second parting. Kai offered her financial security, friendship, and a ready-made family.

There went her hope to get some clarity.

***

Matteo stood near the cliff's edge. Below him, the sea caressed the beach like a lover. He used to swim every day, but whatever had happened six years ago had left him with a dread of water any deeper than a bathtub. He inhaled deeply of the salty air to ease the tension in his soul. Watching Bella drive away with another man had ripped him in two.

In his youth, he would come to this spot every time he was upset and stare out at the Mediterranean, lit now by a moon playing hide-n-seek with the clouds. The sea, his comfort, had become his torment, stealing from him the most precious thing: time.

"Don't jump. You know she still loves you. She's just pissed you were gone so long."

He turned to find Cristoforo standing a few feet away.

"I wasn't going to jump. What do you want, Cristo? Your turn to try and win my wife is tomorrow. She's out with her ex-fiancé tonight."

"I know. I came to see you. Thought you could use a friend." Cristo waved a bottle of grappa but didn't move closer.

"Are you my friend? What kind of man tries to steal his friend's wife?"

"I'm not stealing her. I'm giving her another option. I've cared for Bella for years and believe I can make her happy."

"At the expense of our friendship?"

Cristo shrugged. "If I don't try, I'll regret it for the rest of my life."

They'd been friends since their first day at school and had had each other's backs for years. In competing for Bella's love, Cristo had knifed him in the heart with a jagged blade. But Matteo couldn't blame him. If their situations were reversed, he'd do the same. Didn't mean he had to like it though.

He strode toward Cristo, noting how the other man widened his stance as if expecting a fight but didn't move away.

"What do you know about my disappearance?" Matteo asked as Cristo handed him the bottle of grappa.

"I was in London when you were first reported missing. Your father called me three days after you disappeared, asking if I'd heard from you. I flew straight here and helped in the search. We scoured the beaches and even went to Malta to see if you'd washed up there. The police chief put your description and details in the national missing persons' database and alerted Interpol. However, when the other bodies washed up … well, it was harder to recruit volunteers to hunt for a man they thought was an assassin."

Matteo took another swig of the potent alcohol before passing it back. "Did you think I killed the other men?"

Cristo cleared his throat. "I didn't know what to think. I knew you were desperate, wanting to provide the best for Bella after she gave up everything to marry you. On the other hand, you'd spent your whole life avoiding involvement in the mafia. The evidence was pretty damning, so I thought maybe you didn't want to be found."

"And how long did you wait before you made moves on my wife?"

"I didn't make any moves. After your father died, I moved back to Sicily to help her out. But by then Bella was pretty independent. I urged her to move on, either divorce you for abandonment or have you declared legally dead. But it's only in the past six months that she's been able to even contemplate another man in her life. I was biding my time, waiting for her to be ready."

Matteo's hands fisted. Beating Cristo would probably do more damage than good in his goal to figure out his future. "Tell me about Papa."

Cristo passed back the bottle. "Let's move this discussion someplace more comfortable."

They wandered back toward the house, careful to avoid the sheep droppings. "Did Papa give Bella a hard time after I was gone?"

"No. I think he expected her to pack up and head back to the States. I even heard him suggest it a couple of times, saying he'd call her when you returned. But she refused to go."

"I remember, he thought she'd be like my mother—leave as soon as things got tough."

"Bella has more strength than that."

"I know." His wife had given up her fiancé, her parents, and her rich life in New York to be with him. Now he could finally give her the world, but she didn't seem to want it. Instead, she was tied to a land that had been nothing short of a curse his entire existence.

In many ways, Bella was still the same woman he'd married—warm, caring, ready to laugh. Well, maybe not too much laughter at the moment, but he'd seen genuine amusement on her face when one of the goats had tried to eat a rubber ball. But now she had so many more layers, so much more depth, he was excited to get to know her all over again. The way she'd transformed the farm was nothing short of genius.

How many times had his father told him that this land was the most he could expect in life? Only when the amnesia freed him from that mentality had Matteo been able to reach his full potential. He wouldn't allow a sentimental attachment to a patch of dirt reduce him to a simple farmer once again. Yet that was the man Bella had fallen in love with. The turmoil in his stomach returned.

"Where is Papa buried?"

"Next to your mother."

Matteo's bitter laugh was swallowed by the humid

night air. "You've got to be kidding me." His mother had been killed in a car accident three months after she'd left them, on her way to meet her lover. As the divorce had yet to go through, she'd died a Vanni and been buried with the rest of the family.

"Bella thought it was poetically ironic—your mother wouldn't be able to leave your father's side now."

Matteo's face twisted in a grimace. He hadn't missed what he couldn't remember but his father had never recovered. Papa had never trusted love again. And when Bella had entered their lives, his father had been adamant that his son was repeating his own mistake.

"I need to find out what happened to me. Six years of my life, my marriage, were stolen. I didn't even get to say goodbye to my father."

Cristo stopped walking. "Are you sure you want to know? What if you don't like what you find out?"

The burn in his chest that had started when Bella had told him the circumstances of his disappearance intensified. "No matter how desperate I was, I can't believe I'd execute three men in cold blood."

His friend nodded but took a swig of grappa before answering. "If Bella doesn't choose you ... if she goes back to America with her ex-fiancé or, even better, decides I'm the one she wants, will you be able to walk away?"

A black haze blurred Matteo's vision and his fists clenched once more. Could he watch her leave? The irrational pain in his heart said no. He'd come to see if what they'd had was worth saving or if he should just finish it and move on. He still wasn't certain, but what he did know was that he wasn't going to give up on their marriage without making every effort. "I'm not sure."

"Then be careful what you wish for. Because if it's proved that you killed those men, Bella won't stay with you, no matter how much she loves you. Maybe it's best to let sleeping dogs lie."

"But they're not lying. They're up and barking, hounding our heels. You should have seen the reaction to my reappearance when we went to the village yesterday."

"And the more you stir things up, the worse it will be. Bella's built a successful business now and has a good reputation. You're threatening all that."

The urge to hit something, particularly Cristo, was so strong, Matteo had to close his eyes and count to fifty in Arabic. "If I don't clear my name, this will hang over our heads forever."

"And if it destroys everything Bella has created?"

"I make enough to support her. I've amassed a small fortune in the years I've been away. Have you heard of Polo Properties and Independent African Artisans?"

Cristo whistled. "That's you? Impressive."

"So even if these rumors ruin Bella's ventures—"

His friend was shaking his head even before Matteo finished his sentence. "You don't get it."

"What?"

"The woman you knew six years ago, the one who was happy to play housewife and support her husband, is gone. Bella Vanni now is a determined businesswoman. She runs her various enterprises with every ounce of passion she once poured into your marriage. If you dismiss that, ignore her successes, you've lost her. Doesn't matter who she chooses, it won't be you."

The moon came out from behind a cloud and illuminated the farmyard. Lights gleamed from the windows of the rental cottage. The wool coats of the ewes Bella had separated from the flock and penned earlier in the day glowed, and the camel protested the noises the goats and rabbits made. Only the bees were quiet. All were evidence of his wife's hard work and entrepreneurial spirit.

He'd been raised as a traditional Sicilian male—providing for his wife, protecting her, and being her everything was his mission in life. Now, it seemed that perception needed adjusting as well. "Why are you telling me this? Wouldn't it be more strategic to keep me in the dark?"

"One, because I'm your friend. Two, victory is so much sweeter with a level playing field."

Before he could wipe the smug smile off his so-called friend's face with a well-placed fist, Cristo handed him the bottle and said, "You need this more than me. Tell Bella I'll pick her up tomorrow at five and to wear something super sexy."

This time he did swing a punch, but Cristo easily dodged it. "*Buona notte*, Matteo. If I didn't say it earlier, welcome home."

Cristo climbed into his SUV and, with a salute, left the yard.

Matteo stood in the doorway to the place that had

been home for twenty-six years. Everything and nothing was the same. All the changes, the stress of not knowing where he stood, combined with his recent concussion, gave him a headache to rival the worst migraine he'd ever had. Still, it was nothing compared with the ache in his chest when he contemplated ruining everything Bella had worked so hard to achieve.

Chapter Seven

"Do I dare kiss you goodnight?" Kai asked as he pulled his rental SUV to a stop in front of the cottage.

Matteo sat in a folding lawn chair, his head slumped to one side. A bottle of something had fallen from his fingers onto the ground where the last of its contents had rejoined Mother Earth. Was he passed out? Sleeping? Or just pretending so he could watch them?

If Kai kissed her and Matteo saw, her husband would undoubtedly insist on wiping the taste of the other man from her lips. And that could lead to … well, all kinds of delicious complications. She squirmed in her seat as heat flooded her core.

"Better not. But thanks for an enjoyable evening."

Before she could open her door, Kai took her hand in his. "Think about what I said, Bella. We could have a good marriage."

"I'll think about it. See you Monday?"

His smile transported her back to her twentieth birthday, the day he'd originally proposed. She'd wanted a small, family-only ceremony. Her parents had insisted on a huge, lavish society affair. So before she lost all say in her life, she'd taken the opportunity for a quick trip around Europe while her mother organized the wedding of the century.

The week before she was due to return to New York, Bella met Matteo, or rather crashed into him. Cut off from her family for ruining their dreams, she'd started a new life with Matteo—a happy one until he'd disappeared.

Now she stood at another crossroads, this one with four possible directions.

"I wouldn't miss it for the world." Kai nodded toward Matteo, "Do you need help getting him inside?"

Her gaze returned to her husband, and her heart flip-flopped. How many evenings had she wakened him to come to bed, exhausted after a nonstop day on the farm? But rather than fall back asleep, he'd loved her until she, too, couldn't move. "No. If he doesn't wake up, he can spend the night out here."

Kai laughed. "You're feisty. That's one of the things I've always admired about you. Didn't matter how your parents pressured you, once you made a decision, you stuck with it. It's a quality I want my daughter to have."

"Really? You want your daughter to defy you?"

"Well, maybe not just yet, but when she becomes an adult? I like women who know what they want in life and go for it."

Eight years ago she'd known exactly what she wanted. Now, she wasn't so sure. "What happens when what you want changes?"

He raised her hand to his lips and kissed the back. "You'll figure it out, Bella. I have supreme confidence in you."

Matteo stirred and sat up in the chair. As he rose unsteadily to his feet, her heart lurched again.

"I wish I had your optimism. Because my head and my heart are pulling in two different directions this time." She slipped from the vehicle before Kai could get out. It was probably best to limit interactions between the two men. "See you Monday."

After closing the SUV door, she strode over to Matteo. "Are you drunk?"

He shielded his eyes from the brightness of the headlights as Kai turned around in the driveway. "No. Cristo was here and drank half. But I've got a killer headache."

She winced. As much as she wanted to believe he hadn't been involved in the death of the other three men, the fact was that they were gone. And Matteo was here.

"Put your arm around me. I'll help you to bed."

"Your bed?"

"No."

His groan could have been for her reply or the pain in his head. Once inside she flipped on the overhead light. Looking up at Matteo, his pallor alarmed her.

"I should call Kai back to check you out."

Matteo started to shake his head, but clutched it instead. "No, I don't need a doctor, especially one who'd rather see me dead so he can steal my wife. I just need to sleep."

Weren't you supposed to keep concussion victims conscious? He stumbled and put more of his weight on her. First things first, get him lying down. They managed to make their way to his father's old room without incident, and Matteo flopped onto the bed, flinging an arm over his eyes with a moan.

She turned off the light but opened the curtains to let the moonlight flood the room. "Do you have any medicine to take?" She'd run out of Tylenol last week and had forgotten to buy more yesterday when they were in town.

"In my shaving bag."

She found it on top of the dresser and opened the prescription bottle. The instructions were in Arabic so she had no idea of the dosage. "One or two?" she asked over her shoulder.

"Two." He sounded like he could barely form the word. She ran to the kitchen to get a glass of water so he could take the painkillers.

She managed to prop him up slightly so he could swallow the pills with a drink. Pushing a strand of hair off his forehead, she found it damp with sweat. A cool sea breeze had blown in earlier, so it wasn't warm enough for him to be perspiring. First she'd get him comfortable, then she'd call Kai for advice.

Matteo didn't move while she pulled off his shoes, but when she put a hand to his belt his eyes opened. One corner of his mouth attempted a smile before sinking back into a grimace. "Are you taking advantage of my weakened state?" he asked.

"I'm trying to get you comfortable so you can sleep. Does this happen to you often?"

"Not usually as bad as this. Must be the knock on my head a few days ago." He lifted his hips as she got his belt free. He wanted to take his pants off? She swallowed. By the time she'd removed all his clothes except his boxer shorts, she was sweating. But it wasn't from exertion. His body had always been amazing. Seemed he hadn't lost any of his muscle tone after he left the farm.

"I'll be right back," she said after draping a light sheet over him.

She called Kai, who offered to come and check on Matteo. But if it was just a migraine, it seemed unnecessary to drag him out of his comfortable hotel. "Probably best not to leave him alone. Check his pulse every few hours, and if it's exceedingly fast or slow, call me."

Grabbing a cool, damp cloth and a bottle of lavender essential oil, she returned to the bedroom. Matteo had kicked off the sheet and lay in all his masculine glory in the moonlight. Her own pulse spiked. God, he was gorgeous. How many nights during their marriage had she woken and just stared at him, wondering how she'd gotten so lucky? It was the best car accident she'd ever had.

She ran the cloth over his face and chest, but he didn't stir. Then she poured a drop of oil on the tips of her fingers and massaged his temples gently. His eyelids fluttered as he attempted to open his eyes. "Shush, *mi amore*, relax and let me care for you." She felt as much as heard his sigh of relief. Seconds later, he was fast asleep.

The room was too small for a chair. There was no help for it; she'd have to sleep on the bed next to him. Not wanting to leave him even for the time it took to change in her room, she slipped off her dress then lay down. The mattress dipped where Matteo lay, and she rolled right into him. His arm came around her and she rested her head on his chest. Well, what better way to monitor his pulse than with her ear to his heart. The sigh of contentment that filled the air this time came from her.

God, it felt good to be in his arms.

The tug-of-war within her swung back in favor of her heart. Or was it her body weighing in this time?

The question neither wanted to answer was, how much would she have to sacrifice to have him back in her life again?

***

Matteo woke and stared at the white ceiling, the light from the open curtain blinding him until his eyes adjusted. It was just like waking in the hospital in Tunisia. At least he knew who he was this time. The question was where? The bed was lumpy, and from the ceiling measurements, the room was tiny. A woman wearing only a bra and panties lay draped over him, and a dull throbbing scrambled his brain. No aches elsewhere, though, unless he counted a raging hard-on.

His body was enjoying the soft breast pressed into his side, the silky leg thrown over his thigh, and the dark hair strewn across his chest and down to his belly. He took a deep breath and his nose filled with the scent of lavender and lemon. Bella. Warmth flooded his chest. Had she changed her mind and decided they could sleep together again?

Before his hand could explore, she stirred then sat up with a huge yawn. Her eyes, when they met his, were full of concern. "Some nurse I am, sleeping on the patient. How are you this morning?"

"Good. Better. Best when you were lying on me." He tried to coax her back down, but she shook her head.

"What time is it?" She scooted off the bed and grabbed her phone from the dresser. "Shit. It's already eight. I'm hours behind schedule. Can I get you anything before I go?" She bent down to retrieve her dress and he got a great view of her ass encased in black lace, her full breasts threatening to spill from her bra. His hands clenched on the bedsheets.

"The goats will wait five more minutes. Sit down, *bellissima*. We need to talk about last night." *Or have a proper welcome home—which I hope with all my heart will take longer than five minutes.* But given his present state, he couldn't guarantee it.

She clutched her dress to her chest. "Nothing happened. Kai suggested I check on you through the night to make sure you were okay. Unfortunately, I fell asleep. But you're still alive, so I guess it all worked out in the end." Her gaze darted around the room, never settling on him. A flush infused her skin. *Dio*, was she turned on?

He flung back the sheet, his arousal straining against his cotton boxers. He had a vague recollection of her undressing him last night, but the rest was blank. No way could he have slept through their first time in six long, extremely dry years.

"Bella—"

"I have to go, Matteo. I have a busy day. The vet is coming … and the guy with the ram to service the ewes that didn't get pregnant the first time…"

He stood and ignored the sudden dizziness. He grabbed her wrist as she tried to leave the room. "I just wanted to thank you for looking after me last night."

"I'm glad you're feeling better." She tugged on her arm again and he let her go. She raced to her room and emerged two minutes later wearing jeans and a T-shirt, pulling her hair up into a ponytail as she went.

"I'll make you some breakfast and bring it out to you."

She stopped then, a small smile lifting her lips. "Thank you. Um, I was planning on visiting your father's grave this afternoon. Do you want to come?"

Did he? Not seeing the grave allowed him to pretend, if only for a few more days, that Papa was alive and just on holiday. Not that his father had ever taken a holiday.

"Yes. I'll come. What time?"

"That depends on how horny the ram is. As soon as he's done, we can go."

Merda, now I'm jealous of a ram.

A shower restored some of his mental agility. By the time he dressed and had a breakfast sandwich ready to take out to Bella, another truck had entered the yard. No one had visited the farm when they'd grown vegetables unless it was harvest time. Now it was a hive of activity. In fact, Bella was dressed head to toe in a white protective suit as she removed the frames from one of her bee boxes. In the background, two women clipped flowers from the lavender. The little girl staying in the guesthouse chased one of the rabbits around the fenced-in yard, and a man Matteo assumed was the vet examined Akbar the camel's feet.

Was he hallucinating? Except his imagination wasn't vivid enough to come up with the scene before him.

Bella waved and called out over the noise of the animals, "Don't come near me just yet. I'll be there in five minutes."

When she finally replaced the frames in the hive and had the bees settled, her breakfast had gone cold and the coffee he'd also brought had stopped steaming. Bella removed the large white hat with netting and unzipped her protective suit halfway. She took a huge bite of the sandwich, her eyes closing in rapture as she chewed. He knew a better way to put that look on her face.

"Oh God, this is good, thank you," she said.

Before she could take a second bite, the two young women who had been by the lavender approached, their wicker baskets overflowing with cuttings. Bella tossed a pinch of bread to a chicken that wandered by. Chicken? Where the hell had the chicken come from?

"Matteo, these are my business partners in one of my ventures, Antonia and Bianka. We're called the Lavender Ladies. We make essential oils, soaps, bath salts, and are looking into creating a line of body lotions and hand creams. Ladies, this is Matteo."

His eyes flashed to Bella's as he shook hands with the two young women, neither of whom wore wedding rings and eyed him up like the daily special. Bella hadn't introduced him as her husband. Was that significant?

While the women discussed production schedules,

he laid a possessive hand on Bella's waist. She glanced up at him but made no comment, continuing her conversation about adding a selection of lanolin-based products to their line. Although the other women looked at him curiously, they didn't shrink back or make the sign of the cross, which was progress.

The women said farewell, their eyes full of questions. Before he could ask why she hadn't introduced him as her husband, the vet approached to discuss Akbar's foot condition as well as talk about one of the ewes that didn't seem to be eating. Bella managed to answer his questions and ask educated ones of her own between bites and sips of the coffee. That conversation hadn't ended when an old farm truck lurched into the yard. Bella handed her half-finished coffee to Matteo, wiped her hands on her jeans, and strode with the vet to the truck now parked by the paddock of ewes waiting for their ram lover to arrive.

Matteo stood rooted to the spot, his mind whirling at the transformation in his wife's world. He knew nothing of bees, distilling essential oils, creams and lotions, cantankerous camels, or anorexic ewes. *Dio*, he'd barely been able to follow half the conversations and they'd been in Italian. Cristo was right: if he had any hope of figuring out his heart, he'd have to get to know his wife all over again.

His phone rang, and soon he was pulled into his own world of resort woes and misdirected artisanal shipments. Three hours later, he took a ham and cheese sandwich out to Bella, who leaned against the fence, watching the ram rut one of her ewes. The poor sheep on the end of the amorous activity didn't look amused.

"Oh, thanks," Bella said, a smile in her eyes as she took the sandwich from him. How many times had she brought lunch out to him and his father in the field when they'd been too busy to come in to eat? Their roles had been reversed. But there was no way he could do this long term. Could he convince Bella to give this all up and follow his dreams? Was it even fair to try?

But could he walk away from this woman who intrigued him all over again?

How could he stay?

He wasn't finding answers, just more damned questions.

***

Matteo glanced up from his laptop screen as the cottage door opened and a shaft of blinding light preceded Bella. Her jeans were covered in dirt and from the smell, not dirt. Her ponytail was now at the side of her head and her face was flushed. And he still wanted to take her in his arms and never let her go.

"All done?" he asked.

"Yeah, the ram's just smoking a cigarette before they load him back in the truck."

"What?"

"I'm kidding." She glanced at the clock on the wall, the one that had been there his entire life and never once told the time accurately. "I'll grab a quick shower then we can head over to the cemetery. Do you want to take two cars? I can't stay long as I have to get ready for tonight."

"We'll go together. I don't want to stay long

either." Damn the hitch in his throat. His father had been dead for three years. But to him, it was only three days. He didn't want to say goodbye to Papa at all. They'd disagreed about many things in life but never their devotion to each other.

Bella went to put a hand on his shoulder then seemed to realize how dirty it was and pulled it back. He took it in his instead and rubbed it against his cheek. He was starved for her touch. She sucked in a deep breath. "We don't have to go today." Her voice was soft, gentle ... caring. "It's just my routine, the first Saturday of each month."

"No. I need to do this."

"Okay. I'll be ready in about twenty minutes."

True to her word, bang on time she returned to the kitchen wearing a light, flower print dress, low-heeled sandals, and her hair secured in a knot at her neck. She clutched a straw hat in her other hand.

As he shut down his laptop, she said, "I haven't had a second to text Cristo. Did he say anything last night about what time he'd be here, or where we're going and what to wear?"

"He said he'd be here at five and to dress like a nun because he was taking you to see the pope." Cristo's parents were the most pious Catholics in Sicily, maybe all of Italy. His mother went to Mass at least twice a day.

Bella tilted her head to one side and smiled. Not the tight smile he'd seen from her so far, but the full, megawatt, with teeth, grin that set his heart racing. "I wish I'd known that sooner. I sent my habit to the cleaners just yesterday. I guess the pope will have to say an extra prayer for my soul when I show up in my leopard print bikini."

He swallowed, his mind already envisaging Bella wearing the scanty swimsuit, lounging by one of his resort pools, beckoning him with a crook of her finger.

"Let's go before I'm lying next to my father."

His words wiped the smile from her face. Ah *merda*, coming back from the supposed dead had so many linguistic pitfalls.

He drove her little Fiat, not wanting to draw too much attention with the Maserati. During the twenty-minute drive to the cemetery, Bella napped. He parked under the shade of a tree and stared at his wife for a minute. His heart thudded in his chest so loudly, it was a wonder she didn't wake. Taking her left hand, he kissed her bare ring finger to rouse her.

"You don't wear your wedding ring anymore?" He'd never given her a diamond engagement ring because he hadn't been able to afford it. But the band he'd placed on her finger on their wedding day had been in his family for generations, purchased at a time when the Vannis had been prosperous farmers. And every marriage it had symbolized, except that of his parents, had been happy and well blessed. Bella had loved it, saying the history and the combined love it had seen made it more valuable than any diamond he could give her.

And now she didn't even wear that.

Maybe it was because she was always working and didn't want to get it dirty or worse, lose it. Yet she hadn't worn it last night. Of course, she'd been going on a date with another man. But he'd thought that perhaps she'd put it on to go see her father-in-law's grave. Its absence was another stab in his heart.

She rubbed her thumb over her bare ring finger and stared out the window. "I had to sell it to pay for your father's funeral. I'm so sorry. I knew it was important to your family."

He shut his own eyes. She'd been through so much while he'd been gone. It wasn't fair. The lump in his throat was so large, his voice was raw when it did emerge. "You did what you had to do. I'll get you another one. And the diamond engagement ring I promised you."

"Don't bother."

Her words hit him like a truck. Before he could ask her to explain, she grabbed the small pot of flowers at her feet and pushed open the door. She was halfway to the top of the hill before he caught up with her.

"Bella—"

"Don't pressure me, okay?" She stomped on ahead, the plant in her hand shaking so violently there'd hardly be a sprig of greenery on it by the time she got to their destination.

He'd never been to his mother's grave, so had no idea where his father had been laid to rest. Matteo followed Bella as she stomped to the farthest part of the churchyard. In a corner away from all the prominent headstones of the rich families, she stopped. When she leaned down to put the flowers next to his father's small marker, a tear landed on the stone.

"Bella?"

She tried to keep her head down but didn't resist when he put a finger under her chin and lifted her face to him. Another tear escaped and traced a path down her cheek. He caught it with his lips before it could hit the ground.

"I loved that ring. So, so much. I didn't want to sell it, but what could I do? It was the only thing I had left of value. When I slid it from my finger..." The tears came like a torrent now, and she dashed them away with an angry hand. "It felt like I'd given up on you. But I hadn't."

He wrapped his arms around her, and she tucked her head under his chin. Her tears ran down under the collar of his shirt, each one like a trail of acid, etching her sorrow into his skin.

If only she would stay home tonight and let him take care of her, show her that Cristo wasn't the answer to her uncertainty. She'd sacrificed so much for Matteo. It was time he showered her with everything she deserved. He pressed a kiss to her temple as the tears dried up. But she felt too good in his arms for him to let go anytime this decade.

"Matteo Vanni?"

He turned his head at the sound of his name but didn't release Bella. She, however, stiffened in his arms and dropped hers from his back.

"Yes. Who are you?"

The man in the regional police uniform looked vaguely familiar but about ten years older than Matteo, so it was unlikely their paths would have crossed at school. And he'd never had trouble with the law prior to his disappearance as far as he could remember.

The man ignored his question but bowed toward Bella. "Signora Vanni, how are you? You look beautiful as always."

Matteo took a step toward the man, but Bella squeezed his hand and held him at her side. "Matteo, this is the *questore*, Roberto Della Vedova."

Matteo didn't take the chief's outstretched hand. "Have you come to pay your respects to my father's grave, Signor Della Vedova?"

The man's eyes made another leisurely pass over Bella. Matteo clenched his teeth. If he didn't want to spend the next few days in a jail cell, he had to keep his cool. All his paperwork said his name was Mario Barilla, a Tunisian citizen. They could keep him locked up simply on the pretext of confirming his identity.

"I have come to ask you some questions about the events of six years ago. I did not want to visit Signora Bella's farm in case my presence upset her guests."

"Your discretion is appreciated," she said. "However, I don't see what questions you could have to ask. My husband went missing due to a head injury but has now recovered enough to return to us. We should celebrate."

"There are still many questions about his disappearance. And the deaths of the other men."

Bella stepped in front of Matteo before he could speak. "We have had this conversation numerous times, *Questore*. Do you have new evidence to support your claims that Matteo was involved in those unfortunate men's deaths?"

"No," the man reluctantly admitted.

"Then your questions are irrelevant. We are paying respects to our dear Papa within the sanctity of the church grounds. I ask you to leave."

"This is not over, signora. Your husband was on that boat when the other men died. If he did not kill them then he must know who did. I will not rest until I have answers."

This time Bella took a step toward the official and Matteo grabbed her arm. He didn't need his wife to fight his battles, although her passion in defending him was heartwarming.

"I'll come to your office on Monday morning," Matteo said.

"No, Matteo," Bella interrupted. Her eyes were full of worry as she stared up at him. Maybe she wasn't so convinced he had nothing to do with the other men's murders.

"That will be acceptable. I will expect you at 10:00 a.m., Signor Vanni." The *questore's* gaze once more swept Bella, a leer curling his lips upward. Matteo clenched his fists. No one disrespected his wife.

Before Matteo could strike, the police chief scurried away.

"Have you had trouble with him?" Yet another area where he wasn't around to defend his wife. His list of failures was getting long.

"Not much. I threatened him with a lawsuit if he slandered your name, and he shut up after that. He has no evidence. You don't need to go."

"I have to clear my name, Bella."

She opened her mouth as if to argue so he dropped a kiss on her lips instead. In his mind, Matteo could hear his father clear his throat as he had a million times when they'd turned amorous in his company.

Bella sighed when he released her lips. "Take a

lawyer with you if you insist on going. Cristo can probably give you the name of a good one. I don't trust Roberto Della Vedova. This unanswered crime on his watch means he'll pin the murders on anyone he can find."

"All right. I'll ask Cristo for a recommendation when he comes to pick you up." The reminder of his wife's date left a bitter taste in his mouth.

She checked her watch. "I need to get back to the farm soon. Do you want some private time with your father's grave? I can wait for you in the car."

"I'll come with you." No way in hell was he leaving Bella unattended with the likes of Della Vedova around. And in just over an hour, she'd be leaving him to go out with another man.

Tomorrow, though, was his turn. Forget just a dinner date; he would make it a day she'd never forget.

Chapter Eight

Bella inhaled deeply of the warm evening air. The scent of the night-blooming jasmine from the trellis above mingled with the delicious flavors of the lemon tart on her plate. The flames from hundreds of candles flickered around their solitary table on the roof terrace of Positano's most luxurious hotel. A discreet distance away, a trio played romantic tunes, the lingering notes dancing on the breeze.

She straightened the skirt of her black dress. It was one of the few things she'd brought with her from her old life in New York, but it didn't fit as well as it used to. With her labor-intensive lifestyle, she'd lost at least ten if not fifteen pounds. But it was her sole dressy dress also conservative enough in case Matteo hadn't been joking and Cristo took her somewhere religious. Of course he hadn't. Neither had he complained that the only parts of her skin he could see were from her elbow down and her chin up. It would serve Matteo right if she wore it again at their date tomorrow.

It had taken her most of the private flight from Palermo to Napoli to relax after the scene in the churchyard. She should have known Matteo's return would reach the ears of law enforcement. As she'd hurried to get ready, she'd noticed her husband deep in conversation with Cristo. And, for once, she didn't think Matteo was warning his friend about getting carried away with her. What if the police came and arrested Matteo while she was out? They could make him disappear again. And there'd be no coming back from the dead this time.

"You're thinking about him again." Cristo's deep voice snapped her attention back to her companion. He'd gone to a lot of effort for tonight and here she was mentally with someone else.

"Sorry."

"He'll be fine. Relax. Enjoy yourself for a change. You deserve a night off."

She smiled across her wineglass. What was wrong with her? From the moment a helicopter had landed in her paddock and Cristo stepped out with a dozen red roses, the date had morphed into a fantasy extravaganza. It was something she'd imagined Matteo doing to showcase his newfound wealth.

Tonight was another side of Cristo. He wasn't just her husband's best friend and her shoulder in times of need. He was a man who ran his bank's most successful division and yet remained down-to-earth enough to remember to pick up his mother's favorite chocolate cake every Sunday. Except during Lent, of course, when Signora Bernini gave it up and everyone in the village stayed well clear of her.

Cristo was gorgeous, a man most women would give their shoe collection to be with. His wavy, jet-black hair was brushed back but still curled against the collar of his white shirt. A hand-cut charcoal suit hugged his lean, tie-less form. A sprig of dark hair lured her fingers to open a couple more of his shirt buttons. His green eyes, often lit with laughter, were a surprising contrast to his swarthy skin. As tall and muscular as Matteo, he commanded attention wherever he went.

But the thrill that raced through her whenever her husband came near was absent. Maybe that was a good thing? Matteo had the ability to turn her inside out and upside down with only a smile. It had been thrilling in her early twenties. Now she needed stability—someone she could lean on during hard times. So what if her heart didn't race or her blood pound in her veins when Cristo walked into a room? She'd probably live longer if she didn't put her body under such constant stress.

"How's your dessert?" Cristo leaned across the table and stilled her hand from where it was pleating the tablecloth.

"It's fabulous. Thank you for bringing me here. I've always wanted to visit the Amalfi Coast." The sun was just dipping into the sea, showering the pastel-colored buildings on the hillside with a golden glow. *Webster's* could use a photo of this place in lieu of a definition for romance.

Cristo turned his head to take in the view but returned his gaze to hers. "I've been to this restaurant dozens of times, but only now, with you, does it seem special."

"Dozens of times, eh? That's a lot of women."

He quirked his lips as he realized his slip. "Mostly on business, and any women who came with me were clients or spouses of clients and thus off-limits."

"Oh, come on. There must have been one or two dates you brought here. Convenient, too, with a five-star, discreet hotel downstairs."

His hand tightened on hers. "I'd hoped you'd notice that." His voice dropped suggestively.

She removed her hand from under his. "You know I'm not going to sleep with you."

"Tonight," he added, sotto voce.

She ignored that. "Why have you brought me here, Cristo?"

"To show you what your life could be like if you choose me."

Taking his hand in hers again, she softened her tone. "You will always—"

"Please. Don't tell me I'll always be your friend." He kissed the inside of her wrist. "I've wanted you for years, Bella. Even before Matteo disappeared. I left Sicily because I couldn't stand to see you with him. Then when he was gone… I waited for you to be ready to date again. Waited too long, it seems." A flicker of envy was quickly hidden behind a tight smile. He looked as though he was chairing a meeting and didn't like the results being presented.

"If Matteo hadn't returned, I think, eventually, we could have made a go of it. But now … it would be cheating you if we married."

"How do you figure that?"

"Because you deserve a woman who feels you are her world, the culmination of all her hopes and dreams. For me, you'd be the safe bet, the secure, wise choice. It's not fair to you."

"Bella, I'm in banking. The safe bet is always the

best choice. I could live with being that. Don't discount me yet, *tesori*. Think about what *you* want from life. I'm willing to stay in Sicily. You can continue to run the farm and your other businesses. All I'm asking is to share your life, not take it over. Can the others offer the same?"

He had a point. Kai wanted her to return to America to help raise his daughter. Matteo might not be able to stay in Sicily if the authorities continued to hound him. Even if they didn't, his interests were spread all over the world, and, as he'd already said, he couldn't run his empire from a farm kitchen. And she might not have a business to run if the allegations against him proved true.

Cristo offered her what she'd wanted all along: to share her life, a warm body next to her in bed, companionship…

He kissed her palm again before releasing her hand. He was gallant, caring, warm, and dependable. She could love him, given time—and no Matteo.

Thank God her internet date hadn't worked out or she'd be up to her eyeballs in men.

Complicated didn't even begin to describe her life right now.

***

It was two in the morning before the cottage door opened and Bella tiptoed in. He would pretend to be asleep and not ask about her date. Better yet, he would moan and fake another headache so she spent the night in his bed again.

"Were you waiting up for me?" she asked, spotting him standing in the doorway to his father's old room. So much for that plan.

"I couldn't sleep until I knew you were home safe."

"I was with Cristo. You needn't have worried."

"Bella—"

"Go to bed, Matteo. I'm home. My virtue is intact, and I have to be up in four hours to milk a bunch of ornery goats. I'm going to sleep."

She padded into her room, shoes in hand, and a minute later her bed protested as she flopped onto it. He waited twenty more minutes to ensure she was asleep before he snuck in to turn off her phone and pull the curtains shut. He wouldn't glance at the bed, couldn't peek at her lying there. Because no way in hell would he be able to resist the temptation to crawl in next to her.

He made it to the doorway when she snuffled and turned over, whispering his name with an aching longing. He froze then turned back to look. Bella snuggled the second pillow against her body, fast asleep. He could do better than a pillow, if she'd just let him.

Her bare shoulder and the glimpse of hip where she'd pulled off the sheet confirmed she still slept naked. His cock hardened. It was going to be a short, sleepless night for him.

The next time he heard his name slip from her lips she was stomping across the farmyard, her hair tumbled around her shoulders and down her back, her T-shirt hitched up at one side, exposing her taut midriff, and her feet shoved into a pair of old rubber boots. If she were wearing a designer evening gown he couldn't want her more.

"Did you turn off my alarm and close my curtains?" She came right up to him, her boots toe to toe with his now incredibly disgusting shoes. First thing he was going to buy this afternoon was a pair of farm-friendly footwear.

"Yes." He couldn't stop the grin that formed at her outraged gasp. *Dio*, you'd think he'd eaten her last square of chocolate, spilled her wine, or some equally heinous crime, not given her a few extra hours of precious sleep.

"It's ten o'clock. I'll never get done all I need to. I'll have to cancel our date tonight." She put her hands on her hips, which just stretched her T-shirt tight across her breasts. *Merda*, she wasn't wearing a bra. Her nipples jutted out, begging for his touch. If he weren't holding two very heavy pails of goat's milk, she'd be pushed up against the barn wall, her T-shirt over her head two seconds from now.

"You need more than four hours' sleep to get done all you do in a day. So I canceled your alarm and did your morning chores for you."

She glanced at the pails of milk and then around the yard. The camel was fed and watered and put out in the pasture, a chicken atop his hump, both ignoring the newly milked goats that frolicked nearby. The horse and donkey had been brushed and stood staring at the chicken, no doubt, like him, wondering where on earth that had appeared from. The rabbits had new straw, and the dogs were fast asleep in the shade. He'd done good, if he did say so himself, even though milking had taken him almost two hours rather than the forty-five minutes it took Bella.

"The nannies let you milk them?" She reached for a pail, but he moved back, careful not to slosh his hard-earned liquid. "And when did you learn to milk goats?"

"I Googled it. They were reluctant at first"—he'd been butted and tossed on his ass more than once, and he was pretty sure he'd have a massive bruise on his thigh from where one of the nannies tried to take a piece of him—"but then I discovered they like to be sung to as I massaged their teats. Your goats have very questionable taste in music. They prefer Italian songs about dirty sex."

Bella's eyes widened and a flush crept up her neck. "You sang raunchy songs to my goats as you milked them?"

He hoisted the pails hip level. "Yup, and I got two buckets full. I seem to recall yesterday you got only one and a half."

Her laugh rang out over the farmyard. "I think you've just found your new calling."

If it was making her happy, then yes, he had. "I'll put these in the urn for the dairy to collect. Why don't you go inside and start breakfast? I'll be there as soon as I've had a shower."

"I can—" She reached again for a pail.

"The only way I'm going to let you take this milk is if you agree to shower with me."

The challenge hung in the air between them, and for a second he thought maybe she'd agree. Then she pulled her hand back and shoved it in the pocket of her jeans. "I'll make breakfast."

"Will you do one more thing?" he asked before she could move away.

"What?"

"Unless you want to be ravished on the kitchen table, put on a bra. After six years, I have only so much restraint left."

He turned before she could answer and went to find the empty urn the dairy had dropped off yesterday. Was it wrong to pray for your wife to ignore your request?

***

Bella wiped damp palms down her jeans as she trudged up the hill toward the cottage. Two burly men had arrived, courtesy of her husband, to construct a proper stone fence rather than the wooden one she'd ordered. It would last for years and not need repair. She could have wept to know one task at least was completed right and off her list.

Matteo had done an amazing job on all her chores this morning. Deep down, there was still a farmer in him somewhere. Damn, but she'd have liked to have heard him singing sexy songs to the goats. Maybe she could ask for a reenactment tonight. She wiped her palms again. She was going out with her own husband. Why was she so nervous?

Probably because she'd stood in the kitchen for five full minutes this morning convincing herself that putting on a bra was the wise and sensible thing to do, while her body clamored to shuck all her clothes and wear only the white, lace-edged apron that had been a joke wedding gift from one of her society friends in New York.

But she hadn't. She'd dressed sensibly and cooked breakfast and kept all her clothes on as she sat across from her husband. And spent the whole day wishing to hell she hadn't.

Tonight, however, was another matter. And after last night's latest erotic dream installment, featuring Matteo and a jar of honey, she was as horny as the ram had been yesterday. Having sex with him, however, would sway the jury too far in his favor. She needed to make a rational decision about her future.

Although ... there was a lot of merit in a passionate sex life.

He also hadn't told her where he was taking her. He'd asked about her date last night with Cristo but seemed content only to know where they'd gone and what they'd eaten. She refused to tell him that she'd spent half the time thinking about him.

When she crested the hill, the driveway was full of cars. God, she was not in the mood for a party. Her steps slowed until Matteo appeared at the back of the house. He'd disappeared around lunch, saying only that he'd be back by five o'clock for their date. He still wore his jeans and a navy-blue T-shirt but had new, sturdy boots to replace the handmade leather shoes she'd seen in the garbage can earlier.

She half expected him to whisk her away to some exotic destination and show her his world. After three late nights in a row, she was too tired to even drum up any excitement.

"Have you finished?" he asked, putting his arm around her shoulders and steering her toward the cottage.

"Yes, I got the sheep moved into the other pasture while the men work on the fence."

"Good. Then it's date time. I'll see you in a little bit. Enjoy." He flung open the door to the cottage and ushered her inside then closed it behind her.

She stood for a second in the kitchen. This was her date? At home? Alone? *Like I haven't done that a thousand nights in the past three years.*

"*Buongiorno, Signora.*" A woman dressed in white pants and top gestured Bella into the sitting room. The coffee table had been pushed across the doorway to Matteo's room and a massage table set up in the middle of the empty space.

She'd died and gone to heaven.

The woman massaged Bella for a full hour and a half, liquefying her muscles. She hadn't been so relaxed in, well … ever. When the massage was done, another woman appeared and gave Bella a facial and then applied a little makeup and brushed and curled her hair, leaving it down. Matteo had always loved her long hair. Nowadays it was just easier to pull it into a ponytail and keep it out of the way. Bella couldn't believe the transformation in the mirror. Gone was the exhausted harridan, replaced by the woman she'd been years ago. On the outside, anyway.

"When you're ready," the woman said in a soft voice, "your husband has left a dress to wear on your bed. He's waiting for you at the beach."

She floated from the sitting room to her bedroom,

expecting some sexy little outfit that would barely cover her ass. Instead a long, white, flowing dress lay there, the elasticated neckline was probably meant to wear off the shoulder. One small problem: she had no white underwear. At least the overlay of lace across the top would hide the fact she wouldn't be wearing a bra. Not that she figured Matteo would complain despite what he'd said that morning.

The second problem was whether she had enough muscle strength to make the trek down to the beach. The massage had been so relaxing, all she wanted to do was collapse on the sofa. But when she stepped out of the cottage in her new dress and comfy sandals, her friend Angela's husband, Tony, who occasionally helped around the farm when she needed him, stood next to Akbar the camel. Instead of the drab old rug she'd inherited with him, however, Akbar now stood proudly wearing a bright red and blue blanket and a padded saddle. Estella, the vet's pet chicken, eyed her warily, daring Bella to come near her love.

Tony had the camel kneel as she approached, and, for once, Akbar didn't protest having to earn his keep. Estella plonked herself in Bella's lap as though she were the queen and Bella just added cushioning. This was one for the record books—arriving for a date atop a camel, clutching a chicken. Even for Sicily it was odd.

As she swayed side to side atop the grumpy animal, her body tingled in anticipation of what Matteo had in store for the rest of the evening. He met them at the edge of the beach and, after helping her down, sent Tony, Akbar and his chicken love, back to the farm. He held her hand and just stared. Not that she wasn't equally checking him out.

He'd changed into a white short-sleeved shirt and had left three buttons undone. His tan pants had been rolled up to just under his knees and his feet were bare. She licked her lips; his eyes traced the movement.

"You are so beautiful," he whispered as though he couldn't get his voice to work. "As amazing as on our wedding day."

They'd married here on the beach. Just a few of Matteo's friends and a justice of the peace present because the priest wouldn't perform the ceremony as Bella wasn't Catholic. It had been a beautiful early summer day, one filled with such hope and love. The same sensations flowed through her now. Her chest filled with warmth, and Matteo's hand in hers felt strong and sure.

He smiled. Was he caught up in the memory as well? "Come, eat." He led her over to a small table set up in the sand, a padded bench on one side so they could sit together and watch the waves roll onto the beach. How many evenings had they lain here on a blanket, tracing patterns in the sand, sharing their hopes and dreams?

Matteo placed a bowl of Manhattan clam chowder in front of her before sitting down. The only thing she'd eaten today had been the late breakfast omelet she'd cooked at ten thirty. And even then she hadn't eaten much, too distracted by fantasies of Matteo ravishing her on the table.

"This is so good," she said between spoonfuls. She finished her bowl the same time as Matteo, who she'd often accused of inhaling his food. "Have you been in the water yet?" Because that might just be the perfect end to a perfect date—her husband skinny-dipping while she waited on shore to warm him up.

Matteo froze while getting their second course out of the huge picnic basket a few feet away.

"I don't swim anymore."

"Why not?" He'd been a supreme swimmer, going in every day no matter the temperature of the water or the outside air.

He placed a huge corned beef and pastrami sandwich, worthy of Katz Deli in New York, in front of her. Her mouth watered along with her eyes. He could have tried wowing her with his wealth. Instead, he'd made this date all about her and what she enjoyed.

"I have a water phobia. Even taking a shower is a test." He shook his head and the somber expression on his face was replaced with a sensual smile. "Of course, maybe if I had someone to hold my hand—or other parts of me—I wouldn't be so afraid."

"We'll see," she replied enigmatically. Would the water be warm enough to shower when they returned to the cottage? It was heated by the sun and tended to chill as soon as darkness fell.

At the first bite of her sandwich, she closed her eyes and moaned. This was all the things she missed about New York epitomized in food. When she opened her eyes again, Matteo stared at her with undisguised lust.

"Keep that up and you won't make it to the cheesecake."

She moaned again. Best. Date. Ever.

If ultimate date was the only contest, he won. Hands down.

Chapter Nine

For a very brief second, Matteo considered wading into the cold sea to quell his raging erection. If Bella moaned one more time with that sensuous overtone he remembered all too well, he might explode. She used to make that sound when he flicked her nipples with his tongue. Or ran his hands up the inside of her thigh until he reached her damp panties.

Sitting was no longer an option, so he poured her a large glass of wine instead. He needed a distraction, something to take his mind off her creamy shoulders exposed in the dress or the way the wind teased the hem and threatened to lift it off her legs and show him heaven.

"Tell me about your businesses," he prompted.

She munched her sandwich and tilted her head to one side, a sign he knew meant she was trying to figure out his angle. She was lousy at card games and he'd won every hand of strip poker they'd ever played. Then again, there really were no losers in strip poker.

"The guesthouse evolved when someone stopped me in the village one day and asked if there was any decent accommodation in the area. They wanted a place to completely relax off the beaten track. We'd often talked about converting the old barn into a house for us, so I thought why not, and rent it out until you returned? It was hard getting a loan from the bank for the renovations, but eventually they agreed."

He had a feeling Cristo had something to do with that. "And sheep farming? No one around here has raised animals in decades."

"I know, right? And the climate is perfect. Plus, Tunisia is just across the water and they love lamb. So it was a no-brainer. And a steep learning curve. I had just about failed when I met a tourist from New Zealand who used to raise sheep. He gave me a few pointers. I still lose a few, especially around lambing time, but I'm slowly building up my flock. I sell the wool to a local knitters' co-op, and I'm looking into extracting the lanolin to use in a new range of creams."

"And the Lavender Ladies?"

"I met them at an entrepreneur tradeshow and we came up with the business together. They harvest the lavender and distill the essential oil and then we make the rest of the products together. Lavender oil is a natural stress reliever and good for other ailments. I rubbed some on your temples when you had the migraine the other night."

He nodded. "Where do you sell your products?"

"At the markets. We take turns manning the stands, although I've been so busy lately Bianka and Antonia have done all that legwork."

"Are the products you have in the bathroom samples of what you sell?"

"Yes."

"Do you produce enough to supply a small hotel or

two? I was thinking of adding a proprietary set of soaps and lotions to my high-end resorts. They'd work beautifully."

Her face lit up. "Really? That would be awesome. I'll talk to my partners. Selling at the markets is a real drag. You have to be there super early to set up and then stay late to take down the stand and all for a few hundred euros a day. But we haven't had much luck getting any of the local shops to carry our line."

"Give me samples, figure out how much you can realistically make each month, and we'll run a pilot program in my hotel in Marrakech. If they're popular with the guests, we'll roll them out to the other resorts. You could also sell larger quantities in the hotel shop if there's the demand."

He could see she was already running numbers in her head. He'd wanted a distraction but not a mental desertion. "What about the bees? Why did you get into honey production?"

"That was kind of a twofold solution. I needed bees to keep the lavender blooming but also for medicinal purposes."

He raised an eyebrow but didn't interrupt. Her business acumen was exceptional. With Bella at his side, coupled with Farrah's artistic genius, they could conquer the world.

"Signor Francisco bought the artichoke field from me just after your father died. Then he, too, passed within six months. A young family purchased the farm but found it as difficult as I did to find buyers outside of the mafia's controlled market. They couldn't sell the farm because no one else would buy the land for what they paid...

"Anyway, they had a teenage boy who suffered from really bad allergies. They'd moved to Sicily to get him away from a rough crowd in Napoli, not realizing this would be another kind of torment for him. I felt bad for them, like I'd handed them my white elephant even though I didn't sell to them directly. I read that eating honey made by local bees helps with allergies. I started with one hive and now have four. To be honest, it's my least favorite business, but the honey always sells out each year and we've started to make candles with the wax, infused with the lavender oil, and those are hot sellers, too. So I can't really afford to give up the bees."

He refilled her glass of wine, unable to stop his smile at her animated and roundabout way of explaining a business decision. "And the boy? Did the honey help?"

"Yup, it was Tony and he married Angela, who runs the café and, I assume, made this delicious dinner."

He nodded. "She was delighted when I asked her to make a traditional New York meal for you. Are you ready for cheesecake?"

She glanced at her plate and seemed amazed she'd eaten the whole sandwich. He was surprised as well. But she was so thin, she could do with putting on a little weight. "Actually, I'm stuffed. Let's go for a walk along the beach first, help me work up a bit more appetite."

He eyed the water, a black haze already tormenting the edge of his mind. Bella took his hand

and pulled him toward the sea. As a wave crashed over his feet, he drew in a shattered breath, trying to hold the panic at bay.

Bella's gaze darted to his. "Sorry. I didn't realize it was that bad." She started to move away, but he held her hand tighter.

"No. I can do this. I won't be controlled by fear." He pulled in another deep breath, the salt air calming him. Or was it Bella's hand in his, the hint of lavender that hung about her? He forced a smile as she still stared at him, concerned. "But no deeper than my ankles."

They strolled along the beach toward the south with Bella between him and the sea, the water barely covering his toes when it flowed onto the shore. At first they walked hand in hand, then Bella slipped her arm around his waist and nestled her body against his. They'd always fit perfectly. When they reached the jagged rocks that separated their beach from the next along the coast, he put both arms around her.

Automatically she tilted her head back for his kiss. Their lips met like it was the first time. Determined to keep it light, to let her make the decision as to how far they'd go, he kept the kiss tentative at first, remembering the feel, the texture, the taste of her. There was still so much unresolved between them. But this—this passion—was never in doubt.

And impossible to resist.

***

A wave crashed around her legs, soaking the bottom of

her dress, but Matteo didn't break the hold he had on her. Was she still on the massage table, dreaming this? He plundered her mouth now. This was no gentle reintroduction to loving. This was a man starved of physical connection. She could protest, but her body was too busy getting reacquainted with his. Her hands roamed up and down his back, one even so bold as to cup his ass and pull him tighter against her. His rigid erection pressed against her belly, and she arched into it, eliciting a moan of pleasure from Matteo.

Finally, he released her lips and trailed his down her exposed neck, nipping at the tendon and then soothing it with his tongue. She dragged in large gulps of air, trying to surface from the riptide of desire sucking her under. Too late. His hand found her tight nipple and caressed it through the fabric of her dress. She no longer wanted to move.

She could die happy in his arms.

Desperate for more skin on skin contact, she ripped his shirt open and feasted her hands on his pecs before subjecting his nipples to the same pleasure he'd bestowed on hers. His moan matched her own as he shoved down the top of her dress, baring her from the waist up.

"*Merda*, Bella, you're not wearing a bra." At least that's what she figured he said, because with her blood pounding in her ears like a drummer on meth and his face pressed against her naked flesh, it was hard to be exactly sure. He took a nipple into his mouth, his tongue flicking her into a frenzy. God, had it always been this intense?

Another wave crashed against her, wetting her

dress to her backside. But as she was more intent on getting Matteo's buckle undone while she still had enough brain power to make her fingers work, she didn't particularly care. Besides, with the heat Matteo was generating in her, the cool water was welcome. She was only surprised she didn't sizzle like lava meeting the sea.

She'd just managed to free his belt, pop the top button, and slide the zipper down on Matteo's pants when suddenly she was soaked head to toe. She would have lost her footing as the sand disappeared under her feet if Matteo didn't have a firm hold on her. She spluttered, moving a sopping strand of hair from her mouth.

Matteo's face was white, and the hand that had been fondling her breast now clutched the rock face next to them.

"Rogue wave," he said. "We'd better move away from the water."

As another wave hit, he grabbed her arm and dragged her as far up the beach as possible. The sand was narrower here; they'd have to move quickly to get to the wider beach where the water wouldn't reach. She pulled the top of her dress back up while Matteo refastened his pants. Then taking her hand, he ran with her along the shore. Despite his fear of the water, he put himself between her and the sea.

"I'm more terrified of losing you than of the water," he said as she tried to switch their positions.

They were both thoroughly soaked by the time they returned to their picnic spot. The beach was wide here and only during the fiercest storms did the waves reach the cliff face.

Matteo pulled a blanket out of a backpack and went to wrap it around her shoulders when he froze. "Bella, are you trying to kill me? You've got nothing on under that dress." His voice was strained, his eyes glued to her body.

"I didn't have any underwear that wouldn't show." She didn't need the blanket now. The heat of his gaze warmed her.

"I can't do this." He tossed the blanket at her and turned his back.

She wrapped it around herself, instantly chilled to the bone. She put a hand on his shoulder. "Can't do what?"

"I can't spend another night in the room next to yours, listening to you breathe and move in your bed with me not there beside you. Either you let me love you or I go stay in a hotel until you've made your decision."

"I—" *Want you so bad I can't think straight.*

He turned but didn't touch her. "Bella, eight years ago we stood on this beach and I vowed to love you, and only you, forever. During the time we were apart, my brain may have forgotten you, but my body didn't. I remained faithful. The ring on my finger told me I'd made a vow to someone and had to live up to that—"

"You haven't had sex in six years?" Her heart began to sing the Hallelujah Chorus. Passionate Matteo had stayed celibate even though he couldn't even remember her name? "I haven't slept with anyone else either."

"I can't tell you how happy that makes me. But

surely you can see how hard it is for me to be so close to you, my wife, and not *be* with you." He wrapped his arms around her, blanket and all, resting his cheek on top of her head. But he held his lower body away from hers. "Think of it this way, *bellissima*: if we'd have known we were going to be separated for so long, don't you think we would have had one amazing night of love before I was torn from you? Let's pretend this is that night."

"A time warp, epic sex night—that's all it will be? You won't refuse to leave if I ask you to, or start a fight if I choose one of the other men who have offered for me?"

He hauled in a deep breath. "I also promised on our wedding day to put your happiness before my own. If being with me doesn't make you happy, I will let you go. But know this, *amore*, leaving you again will be the hardest thing I'll ever do."

God, she so wanted this night with him. But she couldn't put her whole future in his hands just yet. Couldn't give up everything she was and everything she'd worked so hard for. Neither could she deny her body that clamored for his touch. "How about this: we have this one night in celebration of what we shared before. But tomorrow at noon, we revert to what we have now: a fractured marriage with both of us wanting different things."

"Bella…"

She spread his shirt wide and ran her hands up his chest, shrugging off the blanket around her. "That's all I can offer you."

"I hate this negotiation, but I accept your terms."

113

He lowered his head to hers and took her lips in a blistering kiss that left her in no doubt that he was going to use every weapon in his sexual arsenal to get her to change her mind.

She was stronger now. No longer the bright-eyed twenty-year-old who thought that love was all that mattered. This was about sex. A physical release. A joining of two bodies. It wouldn't change anything.

Delusions were so comforting.

Matteo swung her into his arms and took two steps toward the path back to the cottage.

"Wait, what about all this stuff?" she asked. As much as she wanted to get lost in their passion, she had guests to think about. It wouldn't do for them to come down to the beach tomorrow morning and find a mess.

"Tony and Angela said they'd clear up."

"You knew the night was going to end this way?"

A wicked smile creased his lips. "A man can dream. And plan. Now, I think it's time you got out of that wet dress."

"My dress is wet?"

He took another couple steps toward the path, intent on getting his woman where he wanted her.

"Wait," she said. He halted, but the look in his eyes said this was the last time. "I want my cheesecake. Something tells me I'm going to need the calories for later."

He laughed and lowered her to the sand so she could grab the dessert from the picnic basket. Inside, she found a plate of chocolate-covered strawberries and a box she was sure held some of Angela's handmade bonbons. She grabbed those items as well.

Matteo loomed over her, obviously wondering what was taking her so long. She popped a strawberry in his mouth and then handed him the cheesecake and box of chocolates.

"I was going to carry you," he said around a mouthful of strawberry.

"I know, but it will be much faster if we both walk." To prove her point, she took his hand and marched off toward the cottage. Now that she'd made the decision to sleep with him, she wanted to get on with it. She had six years of pent-up frustration and about fourteen hours to release it.

By the time they reached the cottage, they were both breathless. It could be because of the brisk pace or because every few minutes Matteo would step in front of her and kiss her until she swayed against him. The cheesecake took a battering, but she didn't care.

Her gaze swept over the farmyard, noting the animals all put away for the night and the dog guarding the paddock where the ewes slept huddled together. All that was left to do was … Matteo.

Inside the cottage, the massage table had disappeared and the furniture was back in place. Matteo put the cake and confection down, and by the time he'd turned around she'd shimmied out of her dress.

"What do you say we work on that water phobia of yours?"

He was at her side in seconds, pulling his clothes off as he moved. She cranked the shower on to full hot, knowing lukewarm was all she could hope for. But she didn't figure being cold was going to be an issue. She stepped beneath the spray to rinse some of the salt from her hair. Closing her eyes, she jumped a little as Matteo's hard, naked body pressed against her.

"Bella, as much as I want to make this memorable, I don't think I'll be able to last long the first time." His voice was gravelly.

"I don't need memorable. I need hard and fast." She pulled his head down to her chest, one of his hands already fondling her breast, the other teasing the curls at the top of her mound. Low moans and startled gasps filled the air as they reacquainted themselves with each other's bodies.

She sank to her knees and took him in her mouth. He flung his head back, the sound of his roar filling the tiny shower cubicle. "Don't. I can't. I want to be in you," he said between short, drawn breaths.

"All right." She slid her body all the way up his, hooked her leg around his waist, then took him in her hand and rubbed the head of his erection against her opening. He caught her moan with an all-consuming kiss. As she teased him at her entrance, prolonging the pleasure for them both, he wrenched his mouth from hers.

"Are you still on the pill? If not, I need a condom."

She was glad his brain still worked, because she hadn't given a thought to contraception. "No. But this one time…" Her period had ended the day before he'd turned up. She should be safe.

It must have been enough reassurance because he lifted her and pressed her back against the cool tile wall as he entered her inch by glorious, amazing inch. When he was finally fully seated within her, he rested his forehead against hers.

"*Ti amo*, Bella. *La mia bellissima moglie.*" I love you, Bella. My beautiful wife.

"Matteo." It was the only word her brain would form.

He moved slowly within her at first, his eyes never leaving hers. Tears ran down her face to mingle with the spray from the shower.

"Am I hurting you? Do you want me to stop?" His harsh voice was at odds with his tender words.

"Don't. Ever. Stop."

Her command broke his restraint and he plunged into her over and over again. Her ass slapping against the tile wall coincided with the grunts from Matteo. His body went rigid as he orgasmed, his shout of triumph echoing through the small room. She wrapped her arms around him and kissed his neck and collarbone. He reached out an arm to shut off the now-cold water but made no other move to disconnect their bodies.

She was happy to stay like this forever.

"I'm sorry," he said when his breathing returned to normal.

"For what? That was amazing." She pushed the wet hair from his face and caressed his cheek.

"You didn't come. I took my pleasure and didn't give you yours."

She forced his head up so she could see into his eyes.

"You gave me more than pleasure. You made me feel like the most important woman in the world to you. You made me feel powerful, beautiful, treasured. Everything a woman wants to feel in her man's arms.

Thank you."

"You are all that. And more." He kissed her, his mouth telling her beyond words what she meant to him. How could she ever let him go? Give up all this for a world of work? She was crazy. But the farm was her safe haven, her home, and deep down she needed to *do*, not just *be*. Matteo wanted to treat her like a princess, put her on a pedestal and worship her. She wanted to get down and dirty and do things. Could they find a compromise?

And what about the accusations that hung over his head like a guillotine with a hair-trigger? Was she willing to gamble everything she'd accomplished on Matteo being able to prove his innocence?

Those concerns were for tomorrow. They still had a lot to do tonight.

He released her lips to trail kisses down her throat and onto her chest. As he took her nipple in his mouth and flicked the taut nib with his tongue, she put all thoughts of the future from her mind. This passion was everything.

"I'll tell you what," she gasped out as he slipped even lower and kissed her belly.

"Hmm?"

His tongue found her center and mimicked the movement his cock had made moments before. "When we're done here, you can sing your goat-milking songs to me. That should make up for…" What the hell did he need to rectify?

He raised his head and seemed satisfied that she could no longer form a coherent thought. "I'll do one better. I'll reenact what I'm singing. But, tesori?"

"Yes?" If both his hands weren't holding her up, she'd be on the floor. Her legs no longer worked, her breathing was erratic, and her heart wanted to do a dance outside her body.

"We're a long way from done here."

Chapter Ten

Bella lay on top of him, their bodies still connected and sweaty from lovemaking. He'd made up for the first time when he'd come too soon by leisurely reacquainting himself with her body and erogenous zones. She'd orgasmed three times before he allowed himself to enter her and lose his mind again. When they'd recovered from that, they'd gone in search of sustenance and ended up making love in the kitchen. They needed another shower, but the water would be freezing. That, and he wasn't sure either of their legs would work.

If he had to choose between living fifty years alone or dying right now, well, he'd go without a regret. There was no way Bella would choose Cristo or Kai. She was his and always would be.

She drew a figure of a heart on his chest with her index finger. "I'm worried about tomorrow."

"About what the others will do when you pick me?"

"That's not it. I'm worried about you going to the police headquarters. What if they lock you up? Maybe you shouldn't go."

"Then they'll just come here. I won't risk your

business."

"What if you went back to Tunisia? I doubt they'll follow. They have no evidence, so they won't be able to get an extradition order."

"I've not done anything wrong. I'm not running." He swept her hair off her face and kissed her forehead.

"You wouldn't be the first innocent man to rot in a jail cell to cover someone else's deeds. Please, don't go."

"They won't arrest me. Cristo and his lawyer will be there. As you said, they have no evidence."

"Matteo…"

He rolled so she lay next to him now and he could see her face. "Bella, I'm no longer a poor vegetable farmer of no consequence. I'm a rich, international businessman with a reputation for fair and honest dealings."

"That's Mario Barilla."

"We are the same person." He put as much confidence into his voice as possible. The fact remained that if he walked into that police station as Matteo Vanni, he was nothing. Bella was correct, all his companies were registered in his assumed name. "Trust me, it will be okay."

She nodded although she still looked worried. "Tell me more about your life," Bella said. "I'm surprised that a man who hated paperwork would willingly tie himself to a life of contracts, meetings, and negotiations. It's almost like you're someone else."

"I am the man you married, just with a larger bank account now." He lifted her hand to his lips and traced his tongue over the veins at her wrist, satisfied when there was a stutter in her breathing. "I've learned to appreciate the administrative side of things now that it's about something that interests me. I guess artichokes and capsicums were never really my thing."

"But how did you get into hotel ownership? You washed up on the beach with nothing. It seems a massive leap to me."

"My first job in Tunisia was at a resort that catered to the European market. But once the tourists stopped coming, the property went into foreclosure. I banded together with some of the other staff and we managed to negotiate with the bank to keep it running until we had the money to buy it. We turned it around so that it relied less on foreign travelers and attracted Tunisians or other wealthy North Africans. I built up my portfolio as other resorts faced similar difficulties. I hold the majority of shares, but the staff all receive stock options once they've completed a probationary period, and a bonus based on year-end profits. That way they're as invested as I am in making the place successful."

"That's impressive. And your artisan cooperative?"

"Four years ago, when redecorating my second resort in Tunisia, I came across a woman who sold ceramic pots in the market."

"Like my Lavender Ladies."

"Yes. But rather than a cottage industry, I wanted to sell the wares to a global market—a very rich, exclusive global market. The profits go to dig wells, set up and staff schools and health centers. Another sum is put into an investment to provide for the artisans later in life, or if, for some reason, they can no longer work."

"That's … amazing." He never wanted her to stop looking at him like that.

"I can't wait for you to see it yourself. In one village, 95 percent of the population were women, as all but the oldest and youngest males had left to get jobs or been forced into the army. They had to walk several kilometers to get water, which was often tainted, and eating only what they could grow, which wasn't much. Farrah taught them to make plates from the local clay and to paint them using the natural resources they had. That was two years ago. Now most of the adult women are making items for us. The death rate has dropped dramatically, and for the first time, everyone, including the artisans, is learning to read."

"Is Farrah the woman you met at the market? I hear you on the phone to her almost every day."

"Yes. She's my business partner in this venture. I'd like for you to meet her. You're both incredible women. I think you'll get along."

"Even though she's in love you." It was a statement, not a question.

"Why do you say that?"

"I can tell by the way you speak to her. I may not understand the words, but I know the tone of voice. There's more than just a business relationship going on."

He took a moment to consider his answer. "Farrah claims to love me."

Bella's gaze drifted to the far wall. "If this doesn't work out with us—"

"Don't think it. Farrah deserves more than a man who considers her a consolation prize. And I could never love her the way I love you."

Rather than smile, Bella shrugged. "I told Cristo the same and he said it would be enough."

Matteo's stomach clenched at the images assaulting his mind: Cristo and Bella lying here like this, naked, satiated after three rounds of loving, discussing the future, a family.

Dio, how would he ever walk away if she asked him to?

"I love you, *bellissima*; we enjoy being together. We had a great marriage. I don't understand why you would even consider giving that up for a lesser relationship with someone else."

"We're not having this conversation tonight. This was supposed to be a celebration of what we had, not a review of what we have now." She crawled from the bed, grabbed her wrap from a hook on the wall, and left the room.

He caught up with her in the kitchen. She'd put the kettle in the sink and stood staring blindly out the window. The kettle was overflowing, but Bella ignored it. Shutting off the water, he wrapped his arms around her from the back. She held herself stiffly at first, but as he kissed the sensitive skin under her ear, she melted into his embrace.

To see her so anxious ripped a strip off his heart. "For me, it's all the same." He spoke past a lump in his throat. "People change and evolve throughout their lives, and their love adjusts. Our lives may have taken different paths for a while, but that doesn't mean we can't continue what we had."

"What we had no longer exists, Matteo."

"I refuse to believe that. What have the others offered that I can't give you?"

"It's not what they're offering; it's what you're asking me to give up."

He spun her around so he could see her face. "I'm asking you to give up eighteen-hour work days with little or no return. I'm asking you to give up living in a hovel with no hot water after dark. I'm asking you to give up a life full of struggles to live comfortably with a man who loves you more than he can say and needs you more than his next breath. You gave up your entire life—your fiancé, your family, your country, your fortune—to marry me. What I'm asking now is nothing compared to that."

"I didn't sacrifice a single thing eight years ago. I didn't want any of the stuff I left behind. Yes, I'd have liked to have kept my family, but they made the decision to cut me off. But now—now I have something. I've made something of myself. I know to you, mister millionaire resort owner and savior of a thousand women, it may not look like much. But I love this land and I love my animals and I love going to bed at night exhausted from actually *doing* something. I didn't want to be a society wife in New York and I don't want to become one now. I need a purpose. I need this farm."

"How can you love this place, Bella? It takes everything a person has, every last ounce of strength, and leaves them with nothing. Look at my papa. He lost the woman he loved and died with nothing, not even enough money to purchase a headstone. I can't let that happen to you. I won't let that happen to you."

"Your father refused to move with the times. He was too sentimental and wanted to do things the way they'd been done for centuries. I can't believe you want nothing to do with the farm. The man I married loved this land. That's why I can't reconcile our past with our present. For all you say, you're not the man I wed."

He dropped his arms and slumped into one of the kitchen chairs. A couple of hours ago he'd had Bella bent over the table, her breasts in the cheesecake as he took her from behind. Now they were arguing over a bit of dirt. He should have let things lie until tomorrow. But every single second they had this wall between them was too much.

"Bella, I was raised being told this farm was all I'd ever have. That the land was the best I could do. Then a crazy American woman crashed into me and I dared to dream of bigger things. When you gave up everything for me, I swore to myself that you would never regret your decision."

"I haven't, Matteo. Even in my deepest depression after you disappeared, I never once thought of returning to America."

He nodded, his throat too tight for words. He swigged a glass of water until he could speak again. "When I woke in Tunisia, I had no idea who I was, but I think in my heart I knew that you were waiting for me. But I was also no longer shackled by the idea that my future was tied to anything. I was able to create something, build something I'm damn proud of.

Something I can leave for my children to continue, knowing that in some small way, I've left the world a better place than I found it. I can't do that here. This farm will always be a reminder of pain and loss. My mother was right to leave. This place will eat you whole if you stay."

"Your mother wasn't right. If she'd stayed, if she'd supported her husband and loved her son, they could have made a go of it. Like I have. Like we can if we work together. You know, that first year after you left, I would sit on the ground and filter the dirt between my fingers and think, 'Matteo touched this earth.' My tears, my sweat, are part of this now. I can't just walk away. The farm gave me something to live for when I had nothing. I won't abandon it."

"And Kai and Cristo will let you stay?"

"Kai wants me to return to America with him and help raise his daughter. But Cristo has promised that I can stay here and run my businesses."

Matteo stifled a groan. Why couldn't he offer the same? The land had been in his family for generations; he should be the one tied to it. But the thought of spending the rest of his life as a farmer, even with Bella at his side… Could he leave if it meant no Bella?

"So, what are you going to decide tomorrow? As your husband, I have a right to know first."

She plunked down on the chair next to his. "I have no idea."

"Then don't decide tomorrow. This is too important a decision to make based on a few days. Take a month. I'll stay here another two weeks and live the life of a sheep farmer with you. Then you come with me for two weeks and see what my life has to offer. After that, we can decide together what we want, what compromises we are willing to make."

She tilted her head to the side. "That sounds reasonable."

He'd press his advantage while he still had it. "One more thing. For this month, we are truly husband and wife. We share a bed, we share our bodies, we share our hearts and our work. I promise to give my best if you will."

Bella's eyes searched his for a moment. "I promise, Matteo."

He'd bought a month. And two weeks to prove she would enjoy the lifestyle he could now give her.

Provided he wasn't thrown in jail tomorrow and charged with a triple murder.

Chapter Eleven

"Are you sure about this?" Cristo asked as they parked near the dock. "It's still the same crowd, and to them you're guilty, evidence or not. I've no idea what you hope to gain by coming here."

"I'm hoping to trigger a memory, anything to help me figure out what happened to me. I remember going to sleep next to Bella on our second wedding anniversary and then waking in a Tunisian hospital. One entire week of my life is a complete mystery." The band of tension around his chest tightened.

Cristo nodded but pointed at their suits. "We should have come after visiting the *questore*. We're going to stand out like a *calamari* in a boatload of sardines."

"I know, but I want to give this a shot before we see the police. I won't be able to refute what they're saying if I don't know what happened." Matteo got out of Cristo's BMW SUV and took a deep breath of the salty sea air. And coughed. The air smelled so bad he could taste it, like rotting fish served with diesel sauce. But it triggered no memories. As a farmer, he hadn't spent a lot of time at the local docks. Now he remembered why.

Most of the boats were out fishing; only a few remained in port. As they walked to the end of the battered concrete pier, several men came and stood on their boat decks, fierce scowls on their faces, their arms crossed and legs spread. Definitely not the type of guys you'd ask questions.

Bang! A rifle blast filled the air. Matteo stopped and glanced over at Cristo, who also froze. "You okay?" he asked.

"So far. We done here?"

"Yeah, I got nothing." Not even the gunshot had triggered a memory. No way in hell would he risk another crack to his skull. The missing week might remain a mystery forever.

He and Cristo slowly turned to find three men blocking their way back to land. One was holding a recently fired shotgun.

Cristo looked significantly at Matteo's clenched fists. "No fighting. I do not want to get blood on my new Savile Row suit," he said from the corner of his mouth.

"We're not here for trouble," Matteo began. "Just looking for some information."

"You're not welcome here, Vanni," one of the men said. "And if your pretty little wife wants to keep her businesses running, you'd better not come back."

Matteo opened his mouth, but Cristo grabbed his arm, hard, before he could respond to the threat. "Leave it," Cristo whispered. "Retaliating is only going to make things worse for you and Bella. That's the *questore's* nephew. You can bet he'll be on the phone in a second if you make any threats."

Merda. Backing down went against every fiber of his being, but fine. He wouldn't punch that asshole into next week—this time.

"I didn't kill those men." Matteo caught the leader's gaze and refused to blink. "They were my friends. I want justice as much as you do."

The fishermen didn't look convinced, but one of them moved slightly so he and Cristo could pass. Once safely back in the BMW, his friend released a loud breath.

"That was … intense."

Matteo stared at the docks while Cristo backed out of the parking spot. The band on his chest tightened another notch. And although they'd escaped today, the tide of public opinion was definitely against him. The longer he stayed in Sicily, the more he risked his freedom, maybe even his life. Yet he'd promised Bella another two weeks. His stomach clenched. Once again, the farm had become his prison.

"What do you know about Roberto Della Vedova?" Matteo asked as they sped along the road to Sciacca, the region's main town. It was larger than the village where he'd accompanied Bella shopping, so he hoped for some anonymity there.

"He comes from Bagheria, near Palermo, and was made *questore* the day after you disappeared. From the start it was like working with the Secret Service; everything was on a need-to-know basis. Even Bella and your father had trouble getting information out of him. He assured us that he'd issued all the missing person reports and alerted the coast guard and national police of your disappearance, but he refused to show us the paperwork. And once the bodies washed up, he was sure you were guilty of the murders and didn't put much effort into finding you."

The police headquarters, a square cement building with no redeeming architectural features, looked as welcoming as a dumpster.

As they exited their vehicle, a man in his late forties, wearing a suit, approached.

"Matteo, this is Batista Preatori, the lawyer I mentioned." Cristo performed the introductions before entering the police station.

Matteo's heart faltered as he crossed the threshold. Was Bella right? Was he a fool to try to clear his name?

The police station was no friendlier than the docks had been. His confidence in his innocence took a hit. What if he had done it? What if his need to provide for Bella had led him to take the assassination contract?

They were shown into a small, windowless interrogation room with paint chipping off the walls and one chair missing its back. Desperation soured the air worse than the rotting fish at the dock.

The *questore,* wearing his dress uniform as though he were going on parade, strode into the room. In this dilapidated space? Things were not as they appeared here. Matteo's sense of having seen the man before their introduction at the graveyard was even stronger this time. He searched Roberto Della Vedova's face, trying to force his brain to remember their previous encounter.

And came up blank.

Matteo introduced Cristo and Battista and the

questore puffed out his chest. When none of the men on Matteo's side of the table looked impressed, Della Vedova snarled at them to be seated.

The rest of the interview went downhill from there. Questions came hard and fast, none of which Matteo could answer. It was as though he'd already been found guilty and this was his one chance to prove his innocence. Still, all they had on their side of the table was supposition. Aside from a couple of vague accounts that the boat had left harbor with four men, three of whom washed up on shore five days later, they had no real evidence that Matteo had even been on board. The alleged fourth man wasn't known on the docks, and descriptions ranged from tall with black hair to short and bald.

Yet the *questore* was adamant it had been Matteo, even though he had nothing concrete to hold him on.

Matteo strode from the building an hour later and sucked in a lungful of freedom.

"Thank you, Batista, for your assistance," he said.

"I'll be in touch," the lawyer said. "There's something not right here. I'm going to do some investigating."

Matteo nodded. "I'll be at the farm for another two weeks. Then my wife is accompanying me to Tunisia. I'm not sure when I'll return after that."

Cristo frowned but kept quiet.

"My personal advice would be to leave the country as soon as possible," Battista said. "Remaining here will only spur the police to action."

"I promised Bella I'd stay for two weeks."

Batista checked his watch. When he raised his

eyes to Matteo they were full of concern. "I hope you don't regret that promise."

So. Do. I.

Chapter Twelve

She should have roses, shouldn't she? It'd been so long since she'd seen an episode of *The Bachelorette*, she couldn't remember how the men were eliminated. Things were probably done differently here in Sicily. Like a kiss on the cheek and a wish for happiness.

Kai was the first to arrive. "Hello, Pop-Tart," he said as he exited his vehicle. "Have you already gotten rid of the others? Or am I the first to arrive?"

"Matteo and Cristo are at the police station," she replied. A shiver wracked her body.

"Did they arrest Matteo?" Kai looked around as if expecting snipers on the barn roof.

"No, he's gone in voluntarily for questioning."

"Brave man."

"Or stupid." Bella pulled in a deep breath. "I'm sorry, Kai, but as much as I appreciate your offer of marriage, I'm going to have to turn you down again. I owe it to the vows I made to give Matteo another chance. And I love the farm too much to leave it."

Kai wrapped his arms around her in a big hug. "Are the two compatible? I may have got this wrong, but Matteo doesn't look like he's ready to take up farming again."

"I'm not sure he is either. What would you do? If you had to decide between your career or your wife?"

"That's no contest. I'd give up everything except my daughter to have even one more day with Tsion."

She could almost feel his heartbreak beneath her cheek.

"But what if you knew she was going to leave? Wouldn't you want something to keep you sane, a reason to get up in the morning?"

"I have Joy for that. But I see what you mean. Without my little girl, I'd still be curled in a ball, lying on the floor in a pool of my own tears."

"I spent plenty of nights in that condition. I don't think I could survive a second round."

"Do you think Matteo will leave again?"

She nodded, her cheek rubbing against the soft cotton of his polo shirt. "I don't think he'll stay. His life is elsewhere now. But he's going to try farming again for two weeks. Of course, that's all dependent on whether he even returns this afternoon. He could be arrested and charged with murder. It would probably be better if he went back to Tunisia…" Except Matteo had promised her he'd stay on the farm and she knew he'd live up to that, even at the risk of his freedom.

Because she'd asked.

Kai dropped a kiss on the top of her head. "Know that you'll always have a place in my life. If you need anything, even just a hug from an old friend, call and I'll come running."

"Thank you. Sometimes I wonder what would have happened if I'd never met Matteo. If I'd married you and stayed in New York."

"At its simplest, we wouldn't be having this conversation. Don't look to the past, Bella. Embrace the future—with all its uncertainty and possibility. Grab love and don't let go. One of us should have a happy-ever-after."

"We both deserve one. I hope you'll find love again, Kai."

He shook his head, a sadness in his eyes she knew all too well.

They were still hugging when Cristo's SUV lumbered down the drive. Bella squinted, desperate to see if Matteo sat in the passenger seat. The relief that swept through her when she saw her husband's glare was palpable.

She dropped her arms from around Kai and straightened her T-shirt. Matteo was out of the vehicle before it had even come to a full stop. Bella was torn between relief he had returned and anger at this possessive display. Sheesh, you'd think he'd trust her by now. She'd stayed faithful to him for six years. Did he think she'd jump in bed with her old boyfriend while he was gone for a few hours? Especially after last night.

Kai laughed. "Be happy, Bella," he said before striding over to Matteo. Her ex-fiancé shook her still glowering husband's hand before leaning in close to whisper something in Matteo's ear.

Whatever it was, Matteo looked annoyed at first then broke out into a broad grin. He clapped Kai on the back. With a wave, Kai got in his vehicle and drove off.

Cristo, looking a bit miserable, finally exited the

SUV and moved to Bella's side.

"You've decided on Matteo, then," Cristo said with no other greeting.

"We're having a trial reconciliation," she replied. "I'm sorry, Cristo. But I made a commitment to Matteo years ago, and our marriage deserves another shot."

Cristo gave her a wry smile. "I would expect no less of you." After a kiss on her cheek, he got back in his SUV and drove away.

Matteo wrapped his arms around her from the back and dropped a kiss on her temple. "That wasn't so bad."

He hadn't just rejected two close friends. "What did Kai say to you?"

"That if I broke your heart he'd cut out mine with a rusty spoon. But then he congratulated me for putting the just-loved glow back in your eyes and said to keep up the good work." He kissed her. Whether to wipe Kai and Cristo's embraces from her mind or he was just carrying on from last night, she didn't particularly care.

Before they ended up back in bed or on the table, she pulled away from the kiss but snuggled against his broad chest. "How'd it go with the police?"

"Fine." All the tenderness of a moment ago, gone.

"Matteo?" She pulled back so she could see his face.

"It was fine, Bella. I don't want to waste any more time on the questionable *questore*. Let's concentrate on us." His lips caressed hers again, but he didn't deepen the kiss. "*Ti amo*," he said as he nuzzled her hair.

What wasn't he telling her?

***

Bella glanced down her list. Everything had been checked off, but she was reluctant to put down her paper and leave. Her two weeks were up. True to his word, Matteo had helped around the farm, splitting the chores and, without her asking, tackling some minor repairs and improvements that had been on her to-do list for too long.

As in the early days of their marriage, they'd cooked together, bathed together, and make passionate love each night. All those times she'd dreamed of Matteo's return—this was what she'd imagined. Now, in reality, it wasn't quite right.

She couldn't have her happiness at the expense of his. While Matteo had put in a fabulous effort, he was restless—anxious to get back to his businesses. He was no longer content to be a farmer and, in truth, she couldn't see him as one anymore. His custom-made suits hung in the wardrobe, and more than once she'd seen him reach for them first when getting dressed before he'd tugged on jeans and a T-shirt. Phone calls to Tunisia had become longer and more frequent, although at least he'd dropped the lovers' tone when talking with Farrah. And the notes he wrote to remind himself of things no longer had to do with crop rotations and yields but resort repairs and potential villages to approach for his artisan cooperative.

The only thing they hadn't done together that they used to was go into the village. Matteo had stayed on the farm for the entire two weeks, not wanting to risk a run-in with the police or more antagonism from the locals. The lawyer Matteo had hired arrived one afternoon about a week into their trial reconciliation. Matteo had spoken to him out in the paddock, far from any listening ears. When Bella had asked what the lawyer had to report, all her husband would say was that everything was under control and no arrest warrant had been issued for him. Yet. And whenever she broached the subject, he'd tell her he had it all in hand and not to worry. Damn it, hadn't she proved to him by now that she was no princess who needed protecting from the realities of life?

Still, every time a vehicle appeared in the drive, Matteo would stiffen and his eyes would get that wary look she'd come to hate. Unless his situation was miraculously resolved, he couldn't stay in Sicily. Either he'd be arrested or he'd go crazy waiting for the hammer to fall.

"You've checked everything twice, *bellissima*," Matteo said. He stood at the barn door, no longer dressed in jeans and a T-shirt. Now he wore one of his beloved suits, although the top buttons of his shirt were undone and he hadn't yet put on a tie. Her stupid heart did a little fibrillation at how sexy he looked, back in business mode. Then again, he looked sexy no matter what he was wearing—or not wearing at all. That was another part of their marriage that had fallen seamlessly back into place. Their sex life was all she'd remembered and more.

"I just need to—"

Matteo strode toward her. "You need to change and finish packing. You've gone through everything with Tony and Angela. And you've left an instruction manual thick enough to knock out Akbar if he were hit with it."

He took the slip of paper from her hand, his eyes quickly scanning all her neat little check marks. In eight years she hadn't spent a night away from the farm. And now she'd be gone for two weeks. Longer, if Matteo got his way.

Where was the adventurous twenty-year-old who had fled her mother's overzealous wedding plans and toured Europe all by herself, reveling in her first, and potentially last, taste of freedom? Was Matteo right— had the farm sucked the spirit out of her? Or was she just scared to leave what had become her haven during a turbulent time?

"Okay, I'm ready," she said, squaring her shoulders.

By the time she kissed Angela and Tony goodbye twenty minutes later, the worms that had been wriggling in her stomach had become butterflies and her teeth had unclenched enough to allow a genuine smile. The other couple was ecstatic to look after the farm for her. Sure, Matteo had paid them a generous salary. But it was probably more to do with the fact that they lived with Tony's parents and staying on the farm meant they'd have the cottage to themselves.

But as she and Matteo made their way down the driveway, not once did he look in the rearview mirror. He really had said goodbye to the farm.

It was less than two hundred miles and a quick flight on a private jet from Palermo airport to Matteo's house in Tunisia. The door Matteo unlocked in the narrow cobblestoned alley looked unpretentious, the same as the tens of others they'd passed. The blue paint was faded and the brass knocker looked like it had been recovered from the ark. But when he flung the door wide and gestured for her to precede him, a gasp caught in her throat.

The outside door was a portal to a magical world of Arabian treasures. Any second she expected a genie to appear and offer her three wishes. A fountain bubbled in a tiled courtyard. Potted palms, lemon trees, and flowering vines on trellises softened the hardness of the white plastered walls, which towered three stories above where she stood.

"Come. Let me show you around." Matteo took her hand, his smile full of warmth as he led her through a keyhole-shaped entryway.

The floors were covered in white marble, the walls half tiled in blue ceramic, the intricacy of the design stunning. Bella paused to take it all in, her mouth falling open when she saw the ornately carved ceiling.

"It was a ruin when I bought it," Matteo commented. "It took ten craftsmen almost a year to restore. Although I did tone down some of the original decor, keeping the floors simple rather than mosaicked. Still, I think it turned out rather well."

"It's gorgeous. Makes the farm cottage look like a hovel."

Matteo put both hands on her face, his thumb tracing the curve of her lips. "The cottage will always be special because that's where our love blossomed. This house is just a little more comfortable."

Comfortable was an understatement. It was one of the most beautiful homes Bella had ever seen—a virtual palace. *If Mom could see me now, she might not have rejected me for marrying Matteo.* But Bella had never wanted her family to accept her husband because of his potential, rather the fact that he made her happy and loved her.

So, what had changed? Matteo still made her happy. He still loved her. Why wasn't it enough for *her* now?

As if sensing her change of mood, Matteo took her hand once more and led her up the staircase. On the third floor, he opened a door to a massive bedroom. A huge bed was draped in white gauzy curtains, the only punches of color in the space were the bright blue cushions. The bed was fit for a king; the base and four posts had the same delicate carving as the ceiling. It probably wouldn't creak and protest during sex like hers at the cottage.

While she ran her fingers over the polished wooden top of the dresser, Matteo opened a door on the other side of the room. A luxurious bathroom beckoned. A tub. The last time she'd had a bath was the morning after Matteo reappeared, and that was more of a quick rinse. Here she could have a long soak, enjoy a glass of wine, maybe read a book … or entertain a certain hot Italian male. A tear threatened. How sad was her life that the sight of a bathtub made her cry?

Bella plonked down on the daybed set into a small alcove. What did she know of this world? She picked at the fringe of a pillow.

"*Tesori*, what's the matter?" Matteo sat on his haunches before her. With his thumb he wiped away the tear that had escaped.

"I can't compete with this. How can I even ask you to give all this up and live on the farm with me?"

She felt his frustration even though his touch remained gentle. "Bella, *you* don't have to compete with anything. The choice is not between you and a house. But you did promise me two weeks of 100 percent effort to integrate into my world."

Pulling in a deep breath, she forced a smile. "You're right. I'm sorry."

Matteo sat next to her on the daybed and wrapped his arm around her shoulders. "There's nothing to apologize for. And I don't want you to hide what you're feeling from me or pretend to like something when you don't."

"I won't. I like your house—it's beautiful."

"Our house. Come, you must be tired. You were up at five this morning and haven't stopped all day. Let's go get something to eat then early to bed. I have meetings in the morning, but you can sleep as long as you want."

"Can I have a bath before bed?" She slid her hand up his thigh.

A sexy laugh rumbled up from his chest. "Only if I get to wash your back."

"I can agree to that."

He stood and tugged her into his arms. "Of course, if you want to bathe first…"

As his lips descended, his phone rang, the now familiar ring tone that indicated a call from Farrah. Bella tensed. Would he answer it or continue his seduction? He dropped a quick kiss on her lips then reached into his pocket and retrieved his cell.

After the greeting, Bella lost the conversation as it continued in Arabic. She'd have to ask Matteo if he had a phrase book she could borrow. Or maybe she'd download one of those online courses. Matteo's gaze skidded to her. Were they talking about her? She strode over to the bathroom and closed the door.

She might not be competing with the house but the woman on the other end of the phone... Matteo said he didn't love her, but he obviously had some feelings for this Farrah.

Tomorrow, when she was well rested and dressed to impress, she'd get Matteo to introduce her to his business partner. Tonight, however, she'd have to go to dinner as the slightly crumpled sheep farmer. It would be nice to freshen up, but she hadn't seen her bags since she'd claimed them at the airport. The driver had dropped them as close to the house as possible, but the car couldn't make it down the narrow alleyway. She settled for a quick wash and a fluff of her hair.

When she emerged from the bathroom, her suitcases had arrived but Matteo was gone. Opening the bedroom door, she could hear muted voices in the courtyard below. She peered over the balustrade to see Matteo hugging a woman with long, curly, black hair. Bella's stomach joined them three floors below as the woman glanced up. The femme fatale in her husband's arms was the most beautiful person she'd ever seen.

The woman's eyes narrowed when she caught sight of Bella watching them. She whispered something in Matteo's ear before she stepped away from him.

145

This just got real.

***

"Your wife is watching," Farrah said, pulling out of his arms. She tucked a strand of hair behind her ear. She wore the hijab only when traveling in very religious areas. Here in Tunis, she dressed more Western, like today's knee-length floral dress and open-toe sandals.

He wasn't in the habit of hugging his business partner, but the Saks Fifth Avenue buyer had agreed to meet with him in New York next week. To get into the American market would be huge for them, allowing them to expand to more villages, more women in need of work and financial security. More children would now escape poverty.

Of course that would be the moment Bella looked down from the balcony. He turned and gazed up at his wife. Having watched her go on two dates with other men, he knew exactly what was going through her mind.

"*Tesori*," he called up to her, "come meet Farrah."

Bella disappeared, and he held his breath. Would she come down or wait him out upstairs? Should he go to her and reassure her there was nothing between him and his business partner?

He'd just decided to go and check on her when she appeared in the courtyard. She'd changed from the jeans and shirt she'd traveled in to the white dress she'd worn on the beach for their date. *Dio*, what if she was naked beneath the cotton? His mouth went dry, and it took two tries to make the introductions.

"I'm pleased to meet you," Farrah lied.

"Same here," Bella replied.

Was it just his imagination, or was there a definite feline hiss in his wife's response? Although he knew it was wrong, her possessiveness sent a tiny thrill through him.

"Farrah came to tell me some great news. We got the meeting with the Saks' buyer. We're going to New York at the end of next week."

"New York?" Bella did not look impressed.

She hadn't been home since their marriage. Surely, she'd like to catch up with old friends, maybe even attempt a reconciliation with her parents. Now that he was no longer a poor vegetable farmer, they might even look favorably upon him. It was one more thing he could give to Bella: her family back.

"I should let you go," Farrah said. "I just wanted to give Mario, I mean Matteo, the good news in person."

"We were just about to get something to eat," Bella said. "Please join us."

Matteo searched his wife's face. What game was she playing? Was she trying to flaunt their relationship in Farrah's face?

"I'm sure you'd like to be alone," Farrah answered. She took two steps closer to the door.

"No, really, Farrah." Bella moved toward the other woman. "I promised Matteo I would integrate into his life for two weeks. You are very much part of that life. I'd like to get to know you."

Farrah's gaze drifted briefly to his, and he read the uncertainty in her eyes. While it would be nice if his

147

wife and business partner got along, he wasn't holding out much hope for it.

"Thank you for the invitation. I'd like to get to know you, too."

"Excellent." Bella turned to him. "Okay, Matteo. Show us ladies a good time."

There was a devilish twinkle in his wife's eyes that he didn't trust.

He was in serious trouble.

Rather than take his hand, Bella latched on to Farrah's arm. "So, Matteo has told me very little about you. Only that you are invaluable to his business and he met you in the market. How did you get into making pottery? Is it a family thing?"

He trailed behind the two women as Farrah talked about her work. From the back, they were remarkably similar. Bella was a little taller; they both had long dark hair, although Farrah's was black to Bella's brunette. And they had a way of tilting their heads to one side when considering something. But when he looked at his wife, his chest filled with warmth.

They arrived at the restaurant where he'd booked a table for two; thankfully, the woman at the desk was more than happy to switch tables for them.

"What does your family think about you working and traveling with Matteo?" Bella asked as they were seated. She had taken the place on the bench next to Farrah, leaving him to sit across from them.

"My family doesn't know. I ran away from an arranged marriage and haven't been home since."

"From the little I know of your culture, that must have been very hard for you."

"It was. But sometimes you must do something, even though it hurts, because you know if you don't you'll never be able to live with the consequences of inaction."

Goose bumps rose on his skin as his eyes met Bella's. It was not advice he wanted her to dwell on at the moment. He cleared his throat. "In addition to overseeing the artisan cooperatives, Farrah is an artist in her own right. She's compiling pieces to exhibit soon."

Thankfully, the ensuing discussion about art shows and working with clay took them through to dessert, which both women declined. Bella wore the tight smile she used when pretending she enjoyed something, like yet another meal of artichokes and bell peppers. Farrah's eyes held a hint of the longing he usually only saw when she cuddled a child. Despite the air-conditioning, trickles of sweat ran down his back, hidden by his suit jacket.

His business partner was the first to make a move after he paid the bill. "If you'll excuse me, I have some early calls to make tomorrow. Mario—sorry, I'm not sure I'll ever get used to calling you Matteo—do you want me to make arrangements for New York, or will you?"

"I'll do it. It's Bella's hometown, so I'll tap into her expertise."

"Great. Good night, Bella. I'm glad I got to meet you."

"Thank you, Farrah. I enjoyed getting to know you as well."

Bella's gaze followed Farrah until she left the

restaurant. When she turned back to him, there was an odd light in her eyes. "So, what's the real story between you two? You may not have slept with her, but you wanted to, didn't you?"

Could he signal the waiter to bring him another drink? "I may have … at one time … considered a personal relationship with her."

"Before you regained your memory or after?"

He drained the water in his glass. Bella deserved the truth. "I originally returned to Sicily to end our marriage if you hadn't already divorced me in absentia. But from the second I laid eyes on you again, I knew I had to see if that's what I really wanted."

"But you have more in common with her than you do with me. You're a Tunisian businessman, not a Sicilian farmer like I am."

"And when we married, I was a Sicilian farmer and you were an American heiress. Commonality doesn't guarantee a happy marriage and differences don't mean it won't succeed."

Bella's gaze skittered from his, and she traced a water ring on the tablecloth with her finger. "Still, if things don't work out with us, I think you should get together with her. She's nice. I didn't want to like her … but I do."

"Bella, we've had this conversation before. I love you. What I felt for Farrah was superficial. When I'm with you, everything is more intense—flavors, sights, sounds. It's like you're a lens focusing the best things in my life."

Bella's eyes darted around the room before she rubbed her bare ring finger. "Well, thanks for telling me the truth. It would have been easy to lie and tell me there was never anything between you."

He released the breath he'd been holding.

Had he dodged a bullet or loaded the gun?

Chapter Thirteen

Bella put down her book and stretched. Day three of her Tunisian adventure and she was bored. As much as she appreciated the break and the chance to relax and unwind, she wasn't used to being idle. She still woke at six, but rather than get up to milk the goats, she made love with Matteo. Then he'd shower and go off to work while she went back to sleep for a few hours. He had staff to cook and clean so all she'd done was read in the courtyard until it got too hot, then puttered around the house.

Aside from the kitchen, study, and two bedrooms, the rest of the place was only sparsely furnished. There were six more bedrooms, three of which had ensuite bathrooms, two receptions, and an open-air lounge with a padded bench along one entire wall. It was a palace. Shame her princess days were long over.

Maybe she'd wander around the *souk* again. Matteo had taken her there last night and she'd stared, half the time mouth open, at all the incredible goods for sale. Unlike in Sicily where he'd been shunned, here the merchants had called out greetings and best wishes to her husband as he'd passed. Furnishing the rest of Matteo's Tunisian palace could be fun, but she didn't want to put her stamp on the place if she wasn't going to stay. With each passing day, she could see he'd never return to life on the farm.

"Excuse me, *madaam*, visitors are for you," Tariq, the houseboy raced over to tell her. She'd never seen him walk anywhere, and the housekeeper, his aunt, was forever scolding him.

"To see me?" She knew two people in Tunisia, aside from the household staff, Matteo and Farrah. Just then her cell phone rang.

"One minute." She held up her finger to Tariq; hopefully, he'd understand to wait. She'd heard him practicing how to say things to her in English, but he often didn't know what she said to him in reply.

The call was from Matteo—maybe he could shed some light on her visitors.

"Hey, Matteo, there's someone here to see me. Any idea who?"

"They are there already? That was quick. It's two students from the university who are studying biochemistry. I thought they could help you work out the formula for those lanolin-based creams you wanted to try. They have all the ingredients with them. If you need any equipment, just call and I'll have it sent over."

"You knew I was bored, didn't you?"

He laughed. "I guessed. In Sicily I never saw you sit still for more than twenty minutes. But if you're not interested or have other plans, just send them away."

"No. Now's good. Thank you."

"*Perfetto*. I have to visit my resort in Sousse and deal with a minor issue there. Would you like to join

153

me when you're done? I can have a car drive you down; it takes about an hour and a half. We can spend the night."

"Sounds lovely."

"I'll have a driver collect you at five. Enjoy your day, *bellissima*."

"*Ciao*, Matteo."

The two students spoke perfect English and certainly knew their stuff. But they weren't pushy or condescending, listening to Bella's suggestions and trying various combinations of ingredients without complaint. By the time the alarm she'd set for 5:00 p.m. rang on her phone, they had a formula that should work well. Bella couldn't wait to whip up a batch with her own ingredients. Except they were all back in Sicily. She could send the recipe to Antonia and Bianka and let them make the first test samples. But product development had always been her baby. Until she returned, she'd have to settle for deciding how to package their new creams.

Matteo's driver was already waiting to take her to Sousse, so she ran upstairs, changed, packed an overnight bag, and was ready in ten minutes. Expecting a luxury car, like the one that had driven them from the airport to the *medina*, Bella hesitated by the door of the rickety old station wagon.

"It is better to travel discreetly when we leave the city. The terrorist threat is still high," the driver said.

Bella nodded and got in, but her nerves were on edge for the entire journey. They went through three levels of security before she was ushered into the reception area of Matteo's resort. If she did decide to stay with him, would they have a family here with the threat of terrorism so high? Could she let her children go to school wondering if they'd come home each day?

Her husband rushed to her as soon as her foot stepped onto the white marble tiles. He kissed her briefly on the cheek and gave her hand a reassuring squeeze. She'd noticed that public displays of affection were not common, so he was always discreet when they were out.

"How was your trip down?"

"A bit scary when the driver told me about the terrorists," she replied.

"It's sensible to be cautious, but if you stop living, they've won."

True, but how hard was it to put into practice? Another adjustment she'd need to make.

Matteo led her out the back of the reception area to a softly lit garden. The sun had just dipped below the horizon, leaving a blaze of pink and mauve glory. They walked through the garden, past an elegant water feature, until they arrived on the beach. Matteo slipped off his new handmade shoes and rolled up his suit pant legs.

"Feel this sand, Bella. It's like walking on flour."

She took off her shoes and followed him to the water's edge. The sand was incredibly soft, the resort the most beautiful she'd ever seen, Matteo as loving and attentive as she could wish for. She forced a smile while digging her fingernails into her palms to stop the tears.

She was treading water. The university students were excited about their future. She had plans for the farm. But personally? A family, children—did she want to go there? Aside from the first time, in the shower, Matteo always used a condom. If she had his baby, it would bind them together forever. He would never let her take his child from him. Part of her—the stupid, reckless part that had accepted Matteo's offer of marriage within two weeks of meeting him—wanted to be pregnant, to have the decision made for her. But that wouldn't be fair to anyone. If she stayed with Matteo, it had to be because it was what she wanted with all her heart, not because she had no other choice.

She had a week and a half to see if Matteo's life could give her what she needed. If she wasn't happy then she couldn't make him happy and eventually that discontent would kill their love.

Matteo wrapped his arms around her and she leaned her head against his chest.

Finding the strength to walk away, if it came to that, was going to take every ounce of resolve she had.

**

Matteo searched among the grass and mud huts for Bella. They'd arrived at the Western Sahara village two hours ago. He'd been busy inspecting the completed pottery pieces, and Farrah had tried to explain to the women artisans that they were putting too much water into the clay mixture, making the final product too fragile to ship. Farrah stood now, with a child on her hip, supervising a group of women mixing the clay.

But where was his wife? He rubbed the knotted

muscles at the back of his neck with one hand.

This was the latest village they'd added to their roster. The well had been dug for clean water but no school or medical facility built yet. He'd have preferred to show Bella one of their successes, but the work-in-progress had to suffice. If she stayed with him, she could come back a year from now and see the improvement. Then there'd be no doubt in her mind that what he did was important. Too important to give up.

But he didn't have a year.

He swatted at a fly. If only the doubts about his marriage were as easily pushed aside. Bella had done her best to enjoy his lifestyle for the past nine days, but he knew she was restless. She called the farm daily for an update and seemed a little disappointed that everything was running smoothly without her.

He found her ten minutes later in a small hut, surrounded by some of the older children. She was showing them the alphabet on her tablet.

"There's no school," she said when she saw him at the hut's entrance.

"Not yet. Clean water first, then we build a school, then a medical center if there's enough need."

"How long does that take?"

"Usually a year for the school, two for the health care center."

"In the meantime, these children go uneducated?"

"We do the best we can, Bella."

"You have the money. Why can't you just build the school when you put in a well?"

"The well goes in first because that frees up the

time they normally spend walking for water and is also a key ingredient in the product. The money for the school comes out of the profits. So until they produce enough to pay for that…"

"Still…"

"It's the way it's done, *amore*. Come now, we need to be back in Marrakech tonight or we'll miss our flight to New York tomorrow."

Bella rubbed her thumb over her left ring finger. He'd wanted to buy her a new ring, but she'd refused until they resolved their issues. This was her tell that she was upset. She did it every time he brought up New York. It might be a better plan to leave her in Tunis while he went alone to the States. Or have her wait for him in Sicily. Except returning to Italy wasn't an option for him. According to his lawyer, Roberto Della Vedova was very suspicious. The missing person reports on Matteo had never been filed and the investigation into the other men's deaths had barely merited one sheet of paper.

Going on his gut instinct, Batista was sure the *questore* was involved somehow. If not directly, then he was covering for someone. It would take a while to investigate, and until it was sorted, Matteo's return to Sicily would jeopardize his freedom. Della Vedova needed someone to pin the crime on to take the heat off himself. Matteo was the most likely patsy.

He couldn't bear to tell Bella that he might never be able to go back to Sicily. Losing her to the farm was still too real a possibility.

He had five more days to prove to her that their marriage could work. To do that, he needed to find something to keep her occupied, something she was passionate about.

Bella stood and immediately the children began to protest her leaving. She hugged as many as she could before following him out of the hut. She put her hand up to shield her eyes from the harsh sun, so he reached out and popped the sunglasses from the top of her head back down to her nose.

"Is every village like this?" She glanced around at the collection of huts, some in better condition than others. A goat wandered around, tasting anything that didn't move too fast. A few scrawny chickens pecked the ground, more out of something to do than the existence of any food. A woman pounded a few grains with a wooden mallet while singing a mournful song. He didn't understand the language, but it was nothing like the happy songs he'd heard in the villages where they'd already established an artisans' cooperative.

"Too many are. But soon I'll take you to one where we've been working with the women for a while. You'll see the difference we can make."

Three huts down, Farrah handed the little boy back to his mother. The truck driver had already fired up the vehicle, and it lumbered away from the village down the dusty track. Empty.

"I thought we were here to pick up the first load of plates," Bella said.

"They're useless. Not made properly. By the time the shipment got to its destination, it would be a pile of colorful dust. Farrah has retaught them the mixture, and we'll come back again in a few months to see if they've got it right."

"Three months? So these kids won't get a school until when?"

"Eighteen months, maybe two years."

"That's unacceptable—"

He wrapped his arms around her and dropped a kiss on her forehead. "It's better than the alternative. If we didn't come and offer the women employment, there'd be no school at all, ever. Besides, even if the product was acceptable and we could speed up the payments, it takes time to find a teacher willing to come to the middle of nowhere. We're lucky if we can get a newly qualified teacher desperate to pay off some of their student loans. The most they stay is six months, and then we have to find someone else."

"There has to be another way."

The tension in his neck eased. Could this pull her heart from the farm?

***

Bella leaned out of the hotel window in Marrakech. She could see a bit of Jemaa El Fna, the main square, as full now near 10:00 p.m. as it had been when they arrived at five in the afternoon. The pounding of tribal drums was muted, but the smoke from the hundreds of stalls selling grilled meat still lingered in the air.

They'd wandered around a little earlier and had even purchased a Berber carpet from the souk for the cottage in Sicily. Would she be there to enjoy the feel of it under her feet in the winter, or would she be in Tunisia trying to find ways to keep her days busy?

Once she'd let go of her farm mentality, always

thinking about the next thing that had to be done, she'd had fun on this adventure with Matteo. She'd enjoyed soup for breakfast, drank more mint tea than she ever thought possible, and had tears stream from her eyes when listening to a group of women sing even though she didn't understand a single word of the lyrics.

It was an awesome vacation. But not reality.

Matteo strode into the room from the adjoining bathroom with only a small white towel around his hips. His muscles bunched and danced as he rubbed another towel through his hair. He did this deliberately, strutted his magnificent stuff every chance he got, to remind her of what he had to offer. Not that she was likely to forget.

"Did you want to go back out? I can get dressed," he said.

She shut the window and licked her lips. "What are my other options?"

His smile could've set her pants on fire. "We could stay in and play strip poker."

She cocked her head to one side. "Aren't you at a bit of a disadvantage, wearing only a towel?"

"I'm giving you a sporting chance."

"Oh, really?" She'd always let him win before, not wanting to crush his masculine pride. This time it was game on. "Call for the cards, Matteo. I just need the restroom for a minute."

"You're not going to add more clothing, are you?"

"Nope. Just change up some of what I've got on. I'll keep the number of pieces the same."

He raised one eyebrow.

By the time she emerged from the bathroom,

Matteo lounged on the huge divan, two glasses of champagne, the cards and a bowl of strawberries on the coffee table in front of him.

Bella took the chair opposite, sitting primly on the edge. She sipped the champagne while Matteo shuffled the cards and dealt them both five. She bit down on her bottom lip, feigning disappointment as she sorted her hand. Two tens and a handful of smaller cards. She could work with that. When she glanced at Matteo, he looked smugly satisfied.

"I'll take three cards, please." She slid her useless cards onto the table and picked up the ones Matteo dealt. Another ten, an eight, and a two. Matteo took two replacements, his lips twitching upward when he saw his new cards.

Bella forced her mouth into a frown and munched on a strawberry as she pretended to decide what to do. "Can I get one more?" She put the two of clubs on the table and had a moment of trepidation when Matteo decided to keep what he had. Peeking at her new card, she held back her sigh of relief. Another eight. Full house.

"Call." Matteo placed his cards face up on the table. He had a flush.

"Oh, I think maybe I've won this hand." Bella laid her cards down and bit her tongue as Matteo's eyes flashed from her cards to her face and back to the cards again. "I'll take your towel, thank you."

As though still unsure what had happened, Matteo pulled the towel off and handed it to her. He reclined again in all his naked glory. "I don't seem to have anything left to play with."

"I wouldn't say that. I can see something to play with." She waggled her eyebrows.

He burst out laughing. "I meant I have nothing to wager in the card game."

"Orgasms," she blurted out. "For every hand I win, you have to give me one orgasm."

"Now I don't know whether to win or lose." He dealt another round of cards. "I quite enjoy seeing you writhe in ecstasy, knowing I brought you there."

"Hmmm, okay, how about for every round you lose, I put on one more piece of clothing. As an added incentive, I've got on a new lingerie set you haven't seen yet."

"I preferred the orgasm bet, but as I'm sure to win, it's a moot point."

"We'll see," she said, giving him a coy smile as she picked up her cards. It was hard to concentrate with him lying naked across from her. She deliberately lost two hands so she was down to her new bra and panties. A self-satisfied smile curved her lips to see Matteo's cock stand at attention when she pulled her shirt off, revealing the black lace bra that pushed her breasts up until they threatened to spill from the top at any moment.

As Matteo stood to pour them both more champagne, she took his dick in hand until he was hard and his breath came in short, sharp pants.

"Are you forfeiting?" he said when she bent over to take him in her mouth.

With one long lick, she released him. "Never. Is it my turn to deal now?"

She shuffled the cards while Matteo lay down on

the divan. He was on his back, his erection waiting for her to finish what she started. It was a distraction technique, and two could play that game. As he looked at his cards, she trailed her fingers across the top of her breasts and then down to the waistband of her lace panties. His eyes followed the movement.

"I'll have that next," he said, gesturing at her bra.

"You have to win first. And if I win, I'll be putting my shirt back on."

"Not going to happen, *bellissima*. I've already got one very fine pair."

She grabbed her breasts. "So do I."

They exchanged cards three times before Matteo insisted they show their hands. He did indeed have two pair, but she had a straight, so she won that round. With a gleeful laugh, she pulled her shirt back on. The disappointment on his face was priceless.

"Either you've been playing a lot of poker while I was gone or you were losing on purpose before."

She shrugged. "You used to say there were no losers in strip poker."

"That was when I won every hand."

Three rounds and two more glasses of champagne later she was down to her underpants and she'd joined Matteo on the daybed. There was more fondling than card playing going on, and the suits were all blurring together in her hand.

"Ha, I've got a full house. Pass me back my shirt," Bella said. No way her fingers would work well enough to refasten her bra. She reached past him to snag her top, running her hand up his thigh on the way.

His fingers encircled her wrist. "Not so fast, *tesori*,

I've got four of a kind. All aces. Hand over that sexy excuse for underwear."

She stared at his cards. He'd cheated. She'd had an ace earlier in the game—no way he had four of them now. But she was done playing—this game anyway.

Putting extra sway in her hips, she sauntered over to the bed and shimmied out of the lace panties. She perched her ass on the bed and leaned back on her arms.

"We're both naked. Now what?"

He stalked over to her. "Now I deliver that orgasm you won. Or was it two?"

"Two, because you cheated that last hand."

Dropping a pillow on the floor between her feet, he sank to his knees in front of her. "Ah, you caught that. Two orgasms, it is."

He picked up her foot and kissed and licked his way from her ankle to her upper inner thigh. Hooking her leg over his shoulder, he gave the same treatment on the other side. With both her legs over his shoulders, he licked and sucked on her core until she came apart on a wave of bliss.

"That's one," he said with a smug smile when she could focus.

He reached for her again, but she caught his hand against her breast.

"I need a few minutes to recover. Switch positions."

He raised one eyebrow but dutifully sat on the bed while she knelt before him. She stroked and licked him until he moaned with each caress of her tongue. Instead of lying back on the bed though, he had both hands on her breasts, massaging and rolling her nipples between his thumb and forefinger until she ached to have his mouth on her.

He gently disengaged her from his cock and lifted her until she straddled him. His tongue flicked her nipple at the same time he slid into her heat.

"Condom," she managed to gasp as his finger found her clit.

"In a minute. I'll pull out before I come. I need to feel nothing but you."

God, she wanted that, too. She'd thought of going back on the pill, but it seemed too permanent, like she was deciding they'd stay together. Right now, however, she wished she'd listened to her first instinct and they could remain like this forever.

When he pulled out several minutes later, she moaned in disappointment. "I can go back in. Finish the job." His voice was low and husky. "But as we've already rolled the pregnancy dice once, I didn't think you'd want to gamble again."

"No, you're right. But hurry back."

She moved onto her stomach while she waited for him to race to the bathroom to grab the condoms out of his shaving kit. Her whole body hummed, anticipating Matteo's to return. When he did, he pulled up her hips and slid into her from behind. They both moaned with pleasure.

He slowly increased the pace, his cock gliding in and out of her in a sensuous torment. Reaching around, he put one finger on her clit while the other toyed with her nipple. She exploded into a thousand shards of pleasure. Surely, she'd never be the same. How could he do this time and time again? Bring her to one impossible height after another until she had no idea where she even came from.

Matteo pounded into her until his body tensed and he came with a roar that would probably get them kicked out of the hotel if he weren't the owner. He collapsed on top of her, and she reveled in the weight of his body on hers.

"And that's number two," he whispered into her ear. "What do you say we go for a bonus round?"

"I love bonus rounds."

Especially when it might be a limited time thing. Why couldn't she just accept what she had and be happy? She'd laughed and loved more in the past nine days than she'd done in the six previous years. But while the princess treatment was great as a fantasy— what woman didn't want to be pampered?—it wore thin after a while. Like when Matteo took a call from his lawyer and then fobbed her off with an "everything's fine." It wasn't "fine" if her husband was about to be charged with a triple homicide.

And she had this damn New York trip to survive. The peace and quiet of her little farm called to her like a chocolate cake to a dieter.

But that siren song had nothing on the *tick, tick, tick* of the countdown clock. Soon the buzzer would sound and she'd have to decide whether to give up everything she'd worked so hard for to seize a love that had limits.

Chapter Fourteen

Had New York always been this gloomy? Even on a bright summer's day, the sunlight was muted as though the beams of light had better things to do than linger here. Or they'd been appropriated by the Wall Street demigods, and lesser mortals would just have to find their own source of illumination.

"What will you be doing today, *tesori*?" Matteo struggled with his cuff links and she went over to assist him.

"Kai contacted some of my old friends, and I'm meeting them for lunch. Then I thought I'd head over to the Metropolitan Museum and see what's new there. What time do you expect your meetings to finish?" She fastened his cuff links and straightened his tie, more out of a need to touch him than it being crooked. She was home, where she'd been born and raised, but it now felt as foreign to her as the tiny Western Saharan village with the uneducated children.

"Around five. Where do you suggest we go for dinner? What's your favorite place to eat?"

Her favorite was the table in her kitchen in Sicily, after they'd cooked together, sampling and kissing along the way. They hadn't done that since they'd left Italy, and she missed the small domestic chore. Would they ever go back to that? Matteo had a cook in Tunis and it was clear he had no plans to return to the farm.

"I'll find some place and text you the details."

"Will Kai be joining us?" A muscle jumped in Matteo's jaw.

"No, he's in surgery all day. Evidently, he's performing a heart transplant on a two-year-old boy. If you're not busy, we've been invited to lunch with him, his daughter, and his parents tomorrow at 1:00 p.m."

"I'm sure I can make it. Will your mom and dad be there, too?"

She dropped her hands from his chest and wrapped them around herself. "Not as far as I'm aware. Knowing Kai, he'll try a reconciliation, but I have no interest in seeing them again."

"Bella—"

"What time's your meeting with the Saks's buyer? Traffic is a nightmare in this city; you have to allow twice as long as expected to arrive on time."

"My meeting's at ten, so I'll leave in just a minute. Here's a credit card in your name, no limit, so buy whatever you want."

She took the card and flicked the edge with her thumb. Just as she'd dressed conservatively in Tunisia and Morocco in deference to the culture, if she showed up to lunch wearing anything less than a designer dress and ridiculously expensive shoes, she'd be pitied by her New York *friends*.

"Thanks. And good luck with your meeting."

He gave her a lingering kiss on the lips. "It's all just filler until I'm back in your arms."

"Sweet talker. Seriously, though, I hope you get

the contract so those beautiful children can get their schools faster."

"I'll do my best. Have fun." He kissed her again quickly before he hurried from the hotel room.

She needed to get a move on as well; she had appointments for a haircut and manicure before she hit the shops.

When she strolled into Veducci's three hours later she felt like a new woman. And not one she particularly wanted to be. Her hair was styled and fell in soft waves down her back, her makeup was flawless, and she wore a black Donna Karan dress and Prada shoes. So far today she'd spent more money than she had for her wedding to Matteo. And undoubtedly more than enough to build and staff at least one school in North Africa. Her skin crawled with the extravagance.

"Bella!"

Within seconds she was surrounded by a gaggle of women. Some she'd grown up with, some she'd gone to college with, one she had no idea who she was, but she must have had some connection or why would she be here? Unless it was curiosity to see what a Sicilian sheep farmer looked like.

The wine flowed, the fake laughter punctured the air, and Bella was told so many times how beautiful she looked and how amazing her body was, it was like the conversation was on a pre-recorded loop.

"Seriously, Bella, how do you stay in such great shape? Yoga? Or is there some new European fitness routine we haven't heard of yet?" Stephania, a college classmate asked.

Everyone stopped talking and stared at her like she

had a secret that would revolutionize their lives. "I run a farm in Sicily. I get up at 6:00 a.m. and don't stop until I fall into bed at 9:00 p.m."

"Oh. Well. I don't think that will work for me," Stephania muttered while pouring herself another glass of wine.

Bella checked the time on her phone, and Tiffany, the woman next to her, immediately grabbed the device from her hand. They passed her screen saver of Matteo around from woman to woman for inspection.

I could've saved a fortune on clothes and simply handed out photos of Matteo to impress them.

"Enough about me, what do you guys do?" Bella asked, pocketing her phone. She was pretty sure one or two women had texted Matteo's photo to themselves.

Two were married to sports stars Bella had never heard of but who, from the general buzz of approval, were considered amazing catches. Three were married to men in the financial sector, and the one Bella didn't know was the wife of a doctor who worked with Kai. She looked extremely bored and kept checking her phone as though waiting for some call to rescue her. Bella knew the feeling.

There but for the grace of a car accident, go I.

"So, the guy in the photo, is he the same one you left Kai for? I thought he was a poor farmer," Tiffany said. Bella could see the woman mentally totaling up the exact amount of money she'd spent on her outfit, right down to the tax.

She and Tiffany had been in third grade together, so she could probably be considered Bella's oldest friend. Tiffany hadn't called or emailed once since

Bella had moved to Sicily.

"Matteo is the man I left Kai for. He was a farmer, but now he's a businessman. He runs this amazing company that helps out hundreds of women living in poverty and provides them and their villages with clean water, schools, and medical facilities."

"Really? I heard he left you soon after the wedding," Portia chimed in. She was already on her third drink, and as she gestured some of the wine sloshed out of her glass.

Bella forced a smile. She was sure every word she said would be reported back to her mother at some point. "Matteo had an accident and lost his memory. But it's been restored and we're back together." *For now.* Bella gulped down a large swallow of her drink, letting the alcohol burn away the trepidation that rose to choke her whenever she thought of the future.

She glanced around the table. No way could she live this lifestyle, the society wife who lunched and went to all the right events and wore all the right clothes. It might be nice to get dressed up once in a while, but this was no longer her world. Even if the choice were to live the rest of her life alone on her sheep farm, she wouldn't trade places with any of the women around this table.

"I think we should meet him, just to make sure he's real," Portia said. "Who knows, maybe you've moved back in with Mommy and Daddy and just snapped that photo of some guy in the airport on your way home."

Natalie jabbed Portia in the side, but it hadn't stopped her.

Bitch.

"He's real. And he's mine. And I don't particularly care if you believe me or not. I have to go soon. I'm meeting my husband back at the hotel where we'll undoubtedly have an amazing round of hot, sweaty sex before we go to dinner. Then back to the hotel where he'll sing dirty Italian songs to me as he massages my aching feet. Honestly, I forgot how uncomfortable these shoes are. I do not know how you ladies teeter around on them all day every day."

"The heels?" Natalie flashed her own five-inch killer shoes out the side of the table. "You get used to them. No beauty without pain. If you stick around, I can give you the name of my podiatrist. He's uh-maz-ing." There was a general snickering around the table. Seemed Natalie's podiatrist didn't restrict himself to servicing her feet.

Bella waved the waiter over and paid the table's bill. Add another couple grand to what she'd spent today. She might not want to be a society wife, but she sure spent like one. She'd have to apologize to Matteo later. Maybe she'd stop at the lingerie shop on the way back to the hotel and buy something to lessen the blow.

See how easy it was to get sucked back into the lifestyle? The constant one-upmanship killed all good intentions.

"Well, it's been great catching up with everyone. If any of you are ever in Sicily, give me a call. I can always use more hands on the farm." Would she even be in Sicily this time next week? Damn, she really needed to get this sorted out.

"No, thanks. I think I'll stick to liposuction and

Botox," Tiffany said with a snide laugh.

And implants. God, now who's being a bitch? New York did not suit her.

"*Ciao.*" With a wave, Bella left her former friends to talk about her.

She popped into the first shoe store she came across and bought a pair of comfortable ballet flats. Relieved she could walk once again, she wandered to her old neighborhood. On the sidewalk outside of her family home, she thought about knocking and attempting a reconciliation with her parents. But her father would undoubtedly be at work and her mother at the hair or nail salon. She could say hi to the housekeeper, but she didn't want to risk getting Teresa fired if her parents had issued a no-admittance order against her.

Her phone rang and Bella snapped open her purse to answer it. Had her mother spotted her and was calling to tell her to stay away? Or to invite her in? No, her mother wouldn't have this number. Her heart leapt into her throat when she saw it was Angela calling from Sicily. Had something happened at the farm?

"*Ciao*, Angela. What's up?"

"Hey, Bella. How's the Big Apple?" Angela's sweet voice helped clear away the lingering toxicity.

"Full of worms. I should have asked when I spoke to you earlier: did you want me to bring anything back for you?"

"Nah, I got all I need right here." Bella could hear the love in Angela's voice. No doubt Tony sat beside her, holding her hand.

"Everything okay over there?"

"Mostly. The farm and animals are all fine. The vet's chicken refused to go home with him, so I hope you don't mind another addition to the household."

"No, that's fine. I figured it would be impossible to separate Estella and Akbar. Anything else?" She was sure Angela wouldn't call just because Bella had now inherited a lovestruck chicken.

"I'm worried about the family in the guesthouse and need some advice."

"What's the problem?"

"The man and woman fight constantly. He gets drunk and she drives off, not returning until the next morning when it all starts again."

"Are they damaging anything?"

"No. But they have a four-year-old daughter. Last night at 10:00 p.m., she was wandering around the yard. Tony knocked on the guesthouse door, but no one answered so we took her into the cottage and made her comfortable. They didn't come for her until the mother returned at eight in the morning. Should we call child services or something?"

"What did the mother say when she found her daughter missing?" How could a mother leave her child, knowing there was a huge possibility the father would be too drunk to care for her?

"She said she was sorry. The husband's just back from a tour of duty in the army and has some issues. She promised it wouldn't happen again."

Bella stared at her childhood home. Elaborate flower displays flanked the brownstone's front door, masking the hypocrisy inside with a cheery welcome. There was nothing for her here. She walked away.

"Then let's leave it for now. But will you keep an extra eye out for the girl?"

"Absolutely. She's a lovely little thing. Her name is Holly."

"Thanks, Angela."

"No problem. Enjoy yourself, Bella. And if you want more time with Matteo, we're happy to stay and help here for as long as you'd like."

"I'll let you know."

Part of Bella longed to be back on the farm where everything seemed so much simpler. She woke each morning knowing what she had to do. Yes, it was physically exhausting, but also satisfying. One thing she had learned during this time with Matteo was that she needed to keep busy or she risked becoming one of the vapid women she'd just lunched with.

Wandering around the Met had lost its appeal, so she grabbed a taxi and headed back to the hotel, with a brief stop at a discount chain store for the "convince Matteo to come back to Sicily" lingerie. He would likely rip it off her in two seconds so spending more than $10 seemed a waste.

If it worked, however, it would be priceless.

***

Matteo eased open the hotel room door. The concierge had said Bella had returned forty-five minutes ago, laden with bags. If she was having a nap, he didn't want to disturb her.

Exhaustion riddled his body. He'd been awake half the night making love to Bella and the other half tweaking the Saks Fifth Avenue presentation. *Dio*, he'd been counting on an answer today. Especially as he'd promised Bella he'd go to that lunch with her tomorrow, to be on hand in case her parents did show up.

He left his laptop on the coffee table and had his jacket, tie, and shoes off before he got to the bedroom. Unfortunately, Bella wasn't in bed, or the adjoining bathroom either. He retraced his steps and saw the doors open to the outdoor terrace. Lounging in a chair, she wore her short wrap, a martini on the table next to her. With her eyes closed, she hadn't noticed his arrival and he took full advantage of the chance to check out his wife unobserved. She'd had her hair styled; there were a few more layers, one of which caressed her jaw. He could wrap it around his finger as his lips replaced the strand against her skin. Her legs were crossed and the wrap had fallen off her thighs, leaving a tantalizing glimpse of black lace. A breeze ruffled the lapel, showing bare skin on her shoulder. What was she wearing, or not wearing, underneath?

"Hey," she said, her voice soft. "You're back early. How'd it go?"

He sat on the chair next to her. Where her wrap was plastered to her chest, he could see the outline of more lace. "The buyer was impressed but wants to throw something called a pop-up party tomorrow to test consumer reaction."

"That sucks." She passed him a glass of whiskey that was next to her martini. "There's ice in the bucket if you want."

"This is good. How was your day? Did you meet

your friends for lunch?"

She made a face. The same one he'd seen when she lost the toss to muck out the donkey's stall in the barn. "I have nothing in common with them anymore."

It seemed she felt the same way about New York as he did about Sicily. Maybe he didn't need to worry about this visit triggering longings to return for her.

He reached over and fingered the strand of hair at her cheek. "I like your hair."

"Thank you." The huskiness of her voice flooded his groin with heat. He had so much work to do, throwing together a party in a city where he knew no one, and all he wanted to do was lose himself in Bella.

He swallowed another mouthful of whiskey, enjoying the burn down his throat. "Where do you want to go for dinner?" They'd better head out soon, before he devoured her instead.

"Here. Let's order Chinese food and spend the evening watching reruns of *Seinfeld*."

"Really?"

"Yeah. I haven't had Chinese in ages. And with all the traveling, I'm tired. Do you need help with the party?"

He finished his drink and toyed with the silk belt tie to Bella's wrap. One tug and he'd reveal all. "The Saks woman is organizing the venue and catering. I have to sort out the display. She's going to invite the store's VIP clientele. But I'm worried. Who's going to come to a last-minute party on a Thursday night?"

"Lots of people. Friday's the dead night. That's when everyone heads back to their country houses. But I'll spread the word." Bella got a wicked gleam in her eye. "In fact, don't worry about the guest list at all. I know a way to pack the place."

He tugged on her belt and the wrap slid open to reveal a sheer black lace corset. She sipped her martini, acting as cool as gelato. "Can you order the food while I take a shower?" he asked.

"Yup."

When he emerged from the shower ten minutes later, Bella snapped his photo with her phone as he strode into the room wearing only a towel around his hips. She'd refastened her robe, but he knew what lay underneath now.

He was seriously off his game. "How long till the food comes?" He should have made love to her first then had her order dinner. Except he'd been sweaty from running around New York in July heat and needed to wash up. Next time, he'd coax Bella into the shower with him.

"Not long enough," she replied. She snapped another photo.

"This is all yours anytime you want," he said, gesturing at his body. "No need to take pictures."

"They're not for me. They're how I'm going to pack this venue tomorrow night. Your phone has been *pinging* with incoming messages. If you have the location and time, I can get started on inviting people."

He grabbed his phone from the table and scrolled through his inbox. "How are you going to invite people with a picture of me in a towel?"

"No one at lunch truly believed you exist. They'll come just to make sure you're real and that I didn't Photoshop your picture."

"I don't have to wear a towel to this thing tomorrow, do I?" He stalked toward her, cornering her against the sofa.

"No. I want you in a full suit. But they'll fantasize about what's underneath, and it'll drive them crazy."

"Kind of like what you're doing to me right now. I like your lingerie." He undid the belt and slipped the wrap from her shoulders to flutter to the floor. His hands slid up from her waist to just under her arms where his thumbs could rub against her nipples through the lace.

"It's itchy as hell."

"I should get it off you—" Before he could complete his sentence, or take action, the door buzzer sounded, followed by a knock. New Yorkers, so impatient.

Bella bent down and picked up her robe. "You have to feed me first." She shrugged it on as she went to answer the door. While she paid for their meal, he forwarded her the location and time details the Saks's buyer's assistant had sent him. This party idea made about as much sense as a chicken falling in love with a camel, but the buyer had insisted.

He helped Bella unload the two plastic bags of food, searching for the forks. "Um, all they sent was chopsticks. I'll call downstairs for some cutlery."

"Why? What's wrong with chopsticks?"

"I've never used them."

"How did I not know this?" A saucy smile quirked her lips upward and she had her head cocked to the side again.

"I was a poor Sicilian vegetable farmer and then a

Tunisian businessman. So far, chopsticks have not been a part of my life."

"Well, no need to worry. I'll feed you." She pushed him onto the sofa, grabbed a container of food and a set of chopsticks and then straddled him, her knees against his hips, her ass on his thighs.

"Is this the normal way to eat Chinese food?"

"Absolutely."

He leaned forward and kissed her. "I've just found my new favorite cuisine."

She unfolded the top of the paper container and a waft of garlic and soy sauce filled the air. Meanwhile, he unwrapped her for the third time. Although, as she was holding the containers of food, he had to make do with pushing the fabric off her shoulders. Before he could taste her, she popped a piece of broccoli and a sliver of beef in his mouth.

The game was on. If she took too long to feed him, he'd nibble on her shoulder and fondle her breasts. As a result, she dropped quite a bit of food on him, which she invariably ate without the aid of the chopsticks. They hadn't even finished half the beef and broccoli when she switched containers. The spicy noodles were delicious, especially when he pulled them from the paper box and draped them over her chest so he could lick them from her skin.

"Behave yourself, Matteo. We have to eat it hot; it's no good cold and there's no way to heat it up," she said as he suckled her nipple through the lace.

"I was wrong. Chinese isn't my favorite food. You are."

The containers were tossed onto the coffee table.

The lace corset ripped. And the true feast began.

Chapter Fifteen

"Matteo, this place is stunning," Bella said as she entered the gallery.

Judging by the dust and cobwebs, the space had been vacant for a while, which didn't bode well for the success of the party. But shortly after Matteo had arrived at 7:00 a.m., a crew of cleaners got busy sorting things out. A lighting guy had shown up around noon, to position the track lights onto the vases and plates Matteo brought with him as samples.

Last night, after they'd made love and eaten the cold but still delicious food, he and Bella had come up with a plan for the exhibition. She'd convinced him to focus not only on the works of art but on the people who created them. Farrah had emailed over as many photos as they had, especially the before and after pictures of the villages and the children. He'd had those printed onto sheets of translucent plastic and then transferred to glass panels throughout the space. With the image on the see-through background, they were subtle but powerful. As if the spirits of the artisans were here in the room with them.

It had been incredible working with Bella, and although they'd both been up until 4:00 a.m. finalizing details, he was now energized and excited.

"You are what's stunning," he said, kissing her on the cheek. She wore another new dress, this one completely conservative in blue polka dots with a ruffle of navy fabric at the neck and hem. Even her red-edged shoes were polka dotted. She'd pulled her hair up into a loose bun at her nape, and an elegant handbag dangled from her elbow. She fit so well into the New York scene, he had a hard time remembering her in jeans and a T-shirt.

She shrugged off his compliment but kept her hand on his arm as she surveyed the area. "At the last count, one hundred people have RSVP'd to my invite."

"You have a hundred friends?"

"No. I have no clue who most of the replies are. But your photo was very popular. I've seen it on several social media sites as trending with the location of tonight's pop-up party. Don't be shocked if the one hundred turns into five hundred."

"I want people to come to see the pieces, not me."

"Darling, if I'd have posted a photo of a vase, you'd have five people here tonight."

She'd drawled out the *darling* like a true New York society diva. He didn't want her to become one of the brittle people she'd told him about meeting yesterday.

"How did your lunch go with Kai's family? Did your parents show?"

"Lunch was good but brief. Kai and his parents are going to stop by tonight. But not for long because Joy, Kai's daughter, is sick with a cold. She's such a sweet little girl. It's heartbreaking she lost her mother so young. I hope Kai finds love again. He and his daughter deserve happiness."

He searched her face, but aside from concern for a friend, there was no longing there. Slipping his arm around her waist, he led her toward the back of the gallery. Had he known he'd have to put on a show, he'd have shipped more pieces over. And unless additional ones arrived on time, what he'd brought would have to do. The crew had spaced them out throughout the area, but it was still rather sparse. He caressed her cheek and searched her eyes. "And your parents, they didn't come?"

"No. Kai finally told me that they've split. My mother has started working, and my father has shacked up with his mistress of ten years. I'm still wrapping my head around it. My parents had seemed so devoted to each other."

"I'm sorry, *bellissima*." And now, on top of the news of her parents' breakup, she had to hang around a party tonight. "If you want to stay in the hotel and not attend this thing, I understand."

She gave him a faint smile. "And leave you alone with all those ravenous women desperate for some fresh man-meat? I think not."

He kissed her. Let his lips tell her how much she meant to him. He'd have deepened the embrace, but a commotion in the staff-only part of the gallery brought him back to reality. "Sounds like the shipment from London has arrived. I had Farrah send some more samples. I'd better see to their unpacking."

"Of course. I'll let you get to it."

Reluctantly he released her, but before he'd taken

two steps, he turned back. "Oh, Bella, I almost forgot to remind you. Tonight I'm Mario Barilla. We'd been talking to Saks before I regained my memory, and it just seemed easier to stick with that name than explain the whole amnesia thing."

"Until tonight then, Mario."

She blew him a kiss and sashayed out the door. The swing of her hips tempted him to follow. Except there was still a shit-load of work to do.

The days were ticking down on their trial reconciliation; he desperately needed to know that she'd chosen to stay with him. He finally had a plan that might solve all their problems.

Tonight, after this stupid party was over, he'd present it to her.

***

Bella pushed open the gallery door once more and walked into a different world. It even smelled like North Africa. Well, the nice smells anyway: mint, cinnamon, apricots... She spied a few discreet diffusers spread around the area. The space had been stunning this afternoon when she'd stopped by. Now it left her speechless. Berber carpets were scattered on the floor, Moroccan lamps hung in the corners. The vases, plates, bowls, and objects d'art that had arrived from London had all been put into position and displayed like the prized treasures they were. To think that women, desperate to put food in their babies' bellies, scraped together the mud with their bare hands and created such beautiful pieces—it was nothing short of miraculous.

Almost as amazing as the man who stood against the back wall, staring at her like she was the eighth wonder of the world. Last night, he'd been so preoccupied about hosting this party, she hadn't spoken to him about returning to Sicily and the farm once his legal problems were sorted. But seeing how her friends turned out had proved to her that she couldn't just be an executive wife. She had to do something. And more than party planning.

"It's after seven and no one's here," Matteo said, after a brief kiss on her lips. The tension in his muscles was evident through his suit. Exhaustion sat heavy in his eyes.

"Relax. No one comes on time to a New York party." But aside from some of the crew she'd seen earlier in the day, and black-clad wait staff pouring flutes of champagne and arranging trays of canapés, the place was empty. "Where are the Saks people?"

"They came by earlier to check on things and said they'd be back soon." His stomach grumbled, echoing through the quiet room.

"Have you eaten anything today?" she asked.

"Someone brought me a hot dog from one of those street carts, but I can't remember if I ate it or not."

She nodded. What with wondering if her parents might walk through the Andersens' door any moment at lunch, she'd barely eaten either. They hadn't, and she'd wasted a good meal. "We'll have a late supper when we get back to the hotel." Provided she could stay awake long enough to eat. City life drained you even if you did nothing.

"More Chinese?" He winked.

She flicked a piece of non-existent lint off his lapel. He'd changed clothes, out of his ass-hugging jeans and into his best suit, although she'd convinced him to leave off the tie and open a few buttons to show his chest hair. Nothing like a show of masculinity to get the women in the mood to buy. She ran her fingers through his hair a little, just to make it more interesting. The door opening halted any further improvements.

"Bella, darling, unhand that man and introduce me," Tiffany drawled.

And so it began.

Within forty-five minutes the place was full, mostly of women, Bella noted with a wry smile. And they were more intent on meeting her husband than bidding on the pieces. It'd been the Saks's buyer's idea to have a silent auction. Probably so they'd have a better idea how much people were willing to pay for the items.

Kai's parents arrived, giving Bella the perfect excuse to remove Matteo from the clutches of the latest group of women to latch onto him. Her photo invite had seemed a good idea at the time; now it was riling the beast within her.

"Darling, I want to introduce you to Mr. and Mrs. Andersen," she said, elbowing a fake redhead who was trying to slip her business card into Matteo's inside pocket.

"Just so you know, I'm not enjoying this female attention," he whispered into her hair.

Yeah, right. But as she'd seen him flash his

wedding ring more than once, he wasn't encouraging the women to fawn all over him. And she'd started it with her photo of him in a towel. She kissed him full on the lips, marking her territory. "As long as you remember who you're leaving with."

"That was never in doubt."

Bella glanced around the room. The silent auction table was now as crowded as the display area. This might just work. "Has the Saks's buyer arrived yet?" Very odd for the person who had insisted on this shindig to not show.

"I had a text from her five minutes ago saying she's stuck in traffic. Evidently, we should have arranged for valet parking as the whole street is blocked with people trying to get in."

"See, I told you it would be a success."

He smiled down at her although the tension never left his eyes. She tightened her fingers laced with his and steered him toward the bar area.

"So, you're the man who stole our Bella away from us," Henrik Andersen said by way of introduction.

"Yes, sir. Once I saw her, there was no way I was letting her go," Matteo replied.

"As long as you make her happy," Hilda, Kai's mother, added. She didn't bother with a handshake and went straight for a hug. "Bella's like a daughter to us."

A lump formed in Bella's throat. Her family might have abandoned her, but she still had people who loved her, including the man at her side. Matteo wrapped an arm around her waist and dropped a kiss on her temple.

"I'm doing my best, Mrs. Andersen."

"Kai didn't come with you?" Bella asked, looking around for her friend.

"No, he stayed home with Joy. I was going to babysit, but then I saw the photo of your husband and had to come see for myself." Hilda gave Matteo the look that only a woman over sixty had time to perfect—the x-ray vision look that said she could see beyond his suit to what lay beneath. And she liked what she saw.

Kai's father put an arm around his wife's shoulders. "And I came to make sure Hilda didn't stab you in the back, Bella, and try to steal your husband."

"As if I'd do that. Stabbing is so vulgar. I'm more of a slow poison type of woman."

Bella laughed. The sweet, gentle Mrs. Andersen would never harm a soul. She hoped. "Have you seen the displays?" Bella asked. "Make sure you read the stories of some of the women who created them."

"We will," Hilda replied. "Bella told us what you're doing with your company, Matteo. We all admire your efforts to help these women make their lives better."

"Thank you. Please, allow me to show you my favorite piece," Matteo said.

Just then there was a loud crash from the back room. "I'll go check," Bella offered.

She left Matteo to show the Andersens around, and made her way to staff-only area. She smelled the wine before she saw the four cases smashed to pieces, two bewildered catering staff standing over them.

"We needed more wine," the older guy said. "More people than expected have shown up."

She took a step away from the approaching wine wave. "What are they supposed to do, come lick it off the floor?"

"It wasn't stacked properly." Both men retreated from the disaster like they'd just come across a crime scene and weren't sure they should touch anything.

Blame could wait. Without wine, this party would be over before it really began. Bella skirted the growing puddle to see if any remained undamaged. "What's left?"

"One case." Which would last all of ten minutes, based on the current crowd and new arrivals still trying to get in the door.

"How soon can we get more delivered?"

"We can't. This was a last-minute gig. We brought all we had in stock."

"Keep the food going around. And only offer drinks to new arrivals. But don't make a scene. I'll go buy more wine." She turned to the younger guy, who looked like he spent more time honing his muscles than his serving skills. "You, come with me."

"Yes, ma'am."

She sent a quick text to Matteo then searched on her phone for the nearest place that sold alcohol in bulk.

It took ten minutes to buy the wine and forty-five to get near the gallery again, even using the back-alley entrance. If the buyer wasn't impressed, she was an idiot.

Bella dusted off her pants and flung the wrap part of her top back over her shoulder. The outfit had looked so elegant on the mannequin at the store. With the fake gold coins edging the black silk it had a North African vibe to it. It wasn't very practical, however, for lugging a ton of wine around. And it now clung to her perspiration-damp skin, making it feel like ants were tap dancing down her spine. It wouldn't get any better once she reentered the gallery either. With the mass of bodies in there, the air-conditioning had all but given up, raising the heat level to North African midafternoon. If they were going for authenticity, they'd nailed it.

She freshened up her lipstick, praying she looked more alive than she felt, and opened the door into the gallery just in time to see her mother kissing her husband.

What the hell?

***

"Your double standards are showing, Mother," Bella said as she approached.

Matteo's hands were at his side, obviously not participating in the embrace but not pushing the older woman aside either.

"Bella? What are you doing here?" Her mother's shrill voice turned heads.

"Right this second, watching you throw yourself at my husband."

"This is your husband?"

"This is your mother?"

Both spoke at once. Matteo removed her mother's hand from where it still rested on his chest.

"Did you remarry?" her mother asked.

Bella pulled her brows together before remembering. "Mario Barilla and Matteo Vanni are the same man. My man." She briefly explained about his amnesia. "But that doesn't account for why you were locking lips with him. Do you go around randomly kissing men these days?" Her mother had always been so reserved. Bella had hardly ever seen her parents show affection in front of her.

Matteo still looked confused. "How is she your mother? Your last name was Howard before we married. This is Tamara Aquilani."

"Aquilani is her maiden name. How do you know her?"

"She's the Saks buyer I've been dealing with the past few months."

"Mom?"

"Well, I had to find something to do when your father decided that banging a woman twenty years younger than him was more important than our thirty-year marriage."

"So you thought you'd try the same and make out with Matteo … Mario … whatever, an obviously married man?"

"We were celebrating," her mother replied. "We've just had a bid for $5,000 for one of the pieces. And all the others are going way above what we'd even hoped for."

"Congratulations." Her sarcasm was not lost on Tamara, who raised one eyebrow in disapproval.

Bella stared at her parent, waiting for some acknowledgment that the daughter she hadn't seen in eight years stood in front of her. Tamara had dyed her hair a more vibrant shade of brunette, with hints of sienna. There were a few more lines around her eyes, and her mouth still had that pinched look of disapproval Bella remembered oh so well.

She waited for a warm greeting, like she'd received from Kai's mom. She waited for an admission that she'd been wrong in opposing her daughter's marriage. She waited for a smile.

And got nothing.

"Mario," her mother almost purred his name, "it's time we made a speech and thanked people for coming."

"Bella?" Matteo held out his hand to her.

"We don't need her." Tamara's harsh tone stabbed Bella straight through the heart.

"She's responsible for half the people here," Matteo said.

Bella hadn't seen him this annoyed since she drove off with Kai and then Cristo.

"Very well, then." Tamara turned on a heel and moved to the center of the gallery.

"You go. I'll stay here. This is your moment," Bella said when Matteo made no move to follow. She couldn't stand in front of this crowd with her hands shaking, her knees about to give way, and her throat so dry she almost gagged.

He didn't even try to hide his exasperation from her. "We're a team."

"A team?" She forced her voice to remain low so not everyone heard. "A team keeps its players in the loop. They don't drop bombshells like, 'by the way, I've been schmoozing your mother for the past three months, trying to get her to buy my products.' Oh. My. God. You did not get back together with me just to try and gain favor with her, did you? Because you can obviously see that was a waste of time." Her eyes darted around the room. Where was a paper bag when you needed one to breathe into?

Matteo grabbed her elbow and pulled her to the rear of the gallery away from all the guests. "You don't really believe that. You're just blaming me for stuff so you'll have an excuse to leave me. You love a bunch of dirt and animals more than me."

She bit her bottom lip until the pain equaled that in her chest. "The dirt, the animals need me. You don't. You don't let me in. You don't tell me what the lawyer says when he calls. You just want me to stand beside you and be the pretty accessory to your accomplishments."

"I didn't want to upset you. It's my job to protect you. You never complained before when we were together." He ran an agitated hand through his hair.

"When we were first married, I let you princess me because I didn't know my own strength. Now I do. I won't be kept in the dark. I won't be treated like I don't know what I want or need. Unless you're willing to treat me like a 100 percent partner, I'm out. I am a woman. A pedestal can't support me now."

He looked like she'd just carved his heart with a serrated blade. The breath he pulled in was ragged. "Bella—"

A high-pitched squeal preceded a finger tapping on a microphone. Over Matteo's shoulder, she saw her mother in the middle of the room holding a wireless mic. "Mario, where are you?" The sickening singsong voice made Bella's skin crawl.

He closed his eyes for a second and when they opened, determination had replaced the anger. "This conversation is not over," Matteo said. "We'll discuss this as soon as I'm done here."

He let go of her arm, and if she hadn't locked her knees together she'd have sunk down to the floor. *Get it together, girl. Do not let Mother see you cry.*

Looking like he was king of the universe, Matteo leisurely sauntered to the middle of the room, snagging a glass of wine on the way. When he stood next to Tamara, he kept a respectable distance between them.

Her mother began to speak, thanking everyone for coming. Bella forced a smile in case anyone glanced her way. As her mother droned on, Bella shifted so her back was against the wall, helping to hold her up.

"What's your mother doing?" Kai's familiar voice was like a warm drink on a cold winter morning.

"Stealing the spotlight. What else?"

"Why?"

"She's the buyer that Matteo's been trying to woo the past three months. I just found out five minutes ago. She's taking credit for this whole thing." Bella waved her hand around the room, all evidence of her husband's passion and talent, the life he'd led before he remembered her.

"Shit. I swear I didn't know."

"How long have you been here?" Had he seen her argue with Matteo?

"Ten minutes. My parents came home and raved about the collection and said I had to see it for myself.

Pretty impressive."

"Did you put the five grand bid on one of the pieces?"

"No. Do you want me to?"

"No. I'd rather the piece went to someone who really wanted it, not a pity offer."

"I don't pity you, Bella. I admire you. My proposal still stands…"

"So does my refusal. New York and I are no longer compatible."

His eyes swept her up and down, no doubt comparing her to the woman he'd seen at the farm. "Doesn't seem like it. You've been back two days and it looks like you've never left."

She ignored that. "Did you know my mother worked for Saks Fifth Avenue?"

"I heard she got a job, but no one said what or I would have warned you."

"I thought your parents were my parents' best friends."

"Well, after you broke off our engagement, things were a bit strained. Then Mom accidentally discovered that your dad was having an affair. She tried to warn your mother, but Tamara wouldn't hear her out."

"Public perception has always been the most important thing to my mother. Didn't matter how bad things were. As long as everyone else thought we were the perfect family, it was all okay in her eyes."

Kai nodded. "Don't become her, Bella."

She turned to glare at him. "How can you even think that?"

"I see it every day in my line of work. Women

who gave up their dreams for their husbands, who have nothing but lunches and parties in their diaries. They become bitter and jaded, always searching for the next thrill to make them feel alive. Sure, they have the clothes, the shoes, the cars, the nice holidays. But nothing to give them a sense of accomplishment. I'd hate to see that happen to you."

"I have the farm, my animals, my businesses…"

"So you've decided to give up Matteo and stay in Sicily?"

Had she? What Kai said was true. She needed a calling, something to give her life purpose. She couldn't just breeze in and take over from Farrah; that wasn't fair to the other woman. Besides, she had no artistic talent. But neither could she run the farm or her businesses from Tunisia or wherever else in the world Matteo happened to be. And there was the whole issue of him keeping things from her.

Matteo was speaking now; his deep voice, lightly accented by an Italian inflection, mesmerized everyone in the room, not just the women. How easy it would be to just be pulled along with his current. Surrender herself to his will and become the mindless woman she dreaded ending up.

"Matteo deserves to be the first to know my decision," she said, neither confirming nor denying Kai's question.

"Well, always know you have me in your corner. I'd better get home. I've got surgery in the morning. Keep in touch, Pop-Tart."

She sensed Matteo's eyes on her as she hugged Kai and kissed him on the cheek, although her husband never lost a beat in his speech.

Kai eyed the crowd. "It's going to take me hours to get near the door. Now I wished I'd played football in college," he muttered.

"You can leave by the back door. It's quicker."

She showed him through the rear exit. As he turned to wave goodbye one last time, Bella's cell phone rang. People in the gallery were clapping now, so the speeches must be ending. She'd just take this call then return to Matteo's side. What he was trying to accomplish here was more important than her troubled heart.

"Hey, Angela, what's up?"

"It's that family in the guesthouse." There was a wobble in Angela's voice, like she was just barely keeping it together. "The mother left two days ago and hasn't returned. We can hear the little girl crying in the house. The dad shouts at her and she stops for a while but neither of them has been outside since the mom departed. What should we do?"

"Knock on the door and offer to take the girl to the beach or for a ride on the donkey. Use the key if the dad doesn't answer. Just get her out of there and safe. Can you look after her until the mom comes to collect her? I'll be on a flight back to Sicily tonight." This wasn't something she could expect Angela and Tony to deal with. The guests were her responsibility, and if anything happened to that little girl, she would blame herself for not being there. And although the family had booked a two-week stay, they needed to go and get help immediately. No way would soft-hearted Angela or Tony be able to evict them.

"Okay. We'll hold down the fort until you get back."

"Thanks, Ang."

She peeked out the door, hoping to catch Matteo's eye. Except he still stood in the middle of the room, Bella's mom's hand on his arm. Some important looking guy with a camera crew seemed to be interviewing them. Media exposure could be crucial to the success of the venture—more schools, sooner, for the children in Africa. She couldn't interrupt him now with her little domestic emergency and jeopardize everything he'd worked for. But neither could she linger. The last flights to Europe left soon.

She managed to flag down a taxi and direct the driver to the airport. On the way, she tried to compose a text to Matteo. In the end, all she could manage was:

Emergency at the farm. Gone back to Sicily. *Ciao*.

Chapter Sixteen

If there was a punching bag within sight, he'd beat the crap out of it. Provided he could summon enough energy to pull on the boxing gloves. He searched the room for Bella, having finally detached himself from her mother. *Dio*, the woman was a leech. She hadn't even hugged Bella when she'd seen her. If she weren't so critical to the success of their launch in America, he'd have told the cold witch exactly where she could put her collagen-injected lips—and it was no place the sun shone.

Only a few stragglers were left at the party. The catering staff had stopped serving about half an hour ago and the silent auction was now closed. The twenty pieces they'd displayed tonight had netted over $75,000. Perhaps they should do more events like this one. Maybe Bella could oversee that division, as throwing impromptu parties definitely wasn't in Farrah's wheelhouse. Her jab about being the accessory to his accomplishments stung. What more could he do to prove how important she was to him? He'd told her he loved her time and again. That she hadn't said the same to him was the empty well in his soul.

"Have you seen my wife?" he asked one of the catering staff. The man was clearing the gallery of abandoned wineglasses.

"Last I saw, she went into the back room with a tall blonde guy," the server replied.

Kai. He'd seen Bella kissing him during the speeches. But surely she wouldn't have left without saying goodbye first. Yeah, they'd had an argument, but it wasn't their first. They'd always been able to talk things through once they both calmed down.

He pulled his phone from his pocket, but it was dead and he'd left the charger at the hotel room. Maybe she'd returned there.

"Can I borrow your cell phone?" he asked Tamara, who still lingered. By the way she kept fiddling with her necklace and tossing her hair behind her shoulder, she was interested in him. She'd been throwing out lures since they met yesterday. *Merda*, he was her daughter's husband. If that wasn't a deterrent, he didn't know what was.

"Sure. Is there a problem?"

My wife has left me. "No." He tried Bella's cell, but it went straight to voicemail. Either she was out of battery as well or had turned it off. Next he tried the hotel, but she didn't answer the room phone either. "Can you close up here? I need to go." He handed Tamara the phone back.

"I thought we could go for a drink and discuss the contract details," she said, putting her hand on his arm again.

This had to stop. If it all worked out, he'd be dealing with this woman for years to come. "Tamara,

I'm happily married to your daughter. While I appreciate your personal interest in this project, it's just business. Please email me the contract and I'll have my lawyer look over it."

She dropped her hand, but with her forehead so full of Botox he couldn't tell if she was angry or disappointed at his rebuff. "Fine. I'll close up here."

No, "give my love to Bella" or any other indication that she recognized his wife as her daughter. If this was the example she'd grown up with, it was a minor miracle that Bella had turned out so warm and loving.

Back in the hotel room, everything was as he'd left it that morning. Bella hadn't packed and nothing seemed disturbed. A cold chill swept up his spine. What if she hadn't gone willingly? He'd obviously ticked off the mafia in Sicily. Did they have connections here? His hands shook, and it took two tries to get the charger plug into his phone. While he waited for it to get enough juice to restart, he paced the room.

The *ping* as messages hit his inbox was the most welcome sound he'd heard, aside from Bella calling out his name as she climaxed. *Dio*, she may not have said she loved him, but she couldn't have faked every emotion she'd shown over the past month. Until she told him herself that it was over, he'd continue to hope. His father had always said it was his greatest weakness. When his mother had left, Matteo had sat by the front door for three weeks, waiting for her to return, not going inside even to eat, pulling his blanket and pillow into the kitchen so he'd be the first to see her when she returned. She hadn't. He prayed this time his faith would be rewarded.

He grabbed his phone and scrolled through the messages, ignoring the work ones. Finally, he saw the text from Bella. It had to be a serious emergency for her to leave without talking to him. Could he catch her at the airport?

"When's the last flight to Europe?" he asked the hotel concierge, who thankfully answered on the first ring.

"You've missed them all for tonight, sir. Can I book something for you for tomorrow?"

Tomorrow might be too late. "Can you arrange a private jet for me?"

"Absolutely. Destination?"

Matteo's cell began to ring, and the number for the Sicilian lawyer flashed up. "I'll let you know in two minutes whether Palermo or Tunis."

"Very good, sir. I'll get right on it."

Matteo picked up his cell but had to bend over as it was still plugged in. "Batista, give me good news."

"Sorry. My investigations have stirred up a hornets' nest. They've issued an arrest warrant for you. Don't come back to Sicily."

"Bella's on her way. Some sort of emergency at the farm."

"She should be fine; the warrant is for you only. But just in case, I'll have an associate follow her from the airport."

"Thanks. Call me when you have any news."

Matteo called the concierge back and told him to arrange the plane for Tunis. He'd have to figure out some way of getting into Sicily undetected. If whatever had happened was urgent enough to call Bella back immediately, it was unlikely she'd be there only a short time. And the longer she stayed on the farm, the harder it would be to get her to leave again. Was this the end of their marriage?

One of the housekeeping staff came up to help him pack, and within thirty minutes he was in the back of a limo heading to the private airstrip where the plane waited for him.

The contract from Saks arrived in his inbox. Twice the number of units per month they'd discussed and double the suggested retail price. It was an unmitigated success.

Too bad it was overshadowed by Bella leaving him.

***

She was covered in a slick of perspiration, there was chewing gum stuck in her hair courtesy of the child seated behind her on the plane, she hadn't eaten anything aside from a few pretzels in eighteen hours or slept in over thirty. Worse, she missed Matteo so much her chest physically ached. Not wanting to rack up any more debt on his credit card, she'd flown economy class to Rome and then had to endure a half-hour interview by the immigration official on why she was traveling without luggage. Not to mention the fact that the coins on her blouse had set off every metal detector she'd passed through, resulting in pat downs and additional screening.

Finally, she'd made it to Palermo airport only to have missed the last bus to Seccagrande. She either had to rent a car, call someone to pick her up, or spend the night in the Sicilian capital. Last she'd heard from Cristo, he was in Hong Kong, being wooed to take over the Asian division of his bank. Which left Tony or Angela. But when she'd called them from Rome for an update, they were struggling to look after a small child and still get all the farm work done. It wasn't fair to ask them to now come collect her.

Looked like she'd be adding one more expense to Matteo's credit card.

"*Scusi*, signora."

Bella turned to find a man in a suit holding out a phone to her. Her phone battery had died shortly after texting Matteo. She'd had to use a pay phone to call Angela earlier.

"Yes?" She'd been speaking English so much lately she forgot to reply in Italian.

Instead of answering, he thrust the phone into her hand.

She took it but still stared at the man who'd forced the phone on her. Had she met him before? He'd been on her flight from Rome, but they hadn't spoken. "Hello?" she said into the phone.

"Signora Vanni, this is Batista Preatori. Do you know who I am?"

"Yes." Oh God, Matteo hadn't been arrested, had he?

"The man who handed you the phone is working for me. With the authority of your husband, we have been following you from Rome."

"Why? Am I in danger?"

"We think not but I wanted to be sure. An arrest warrant has been issued for your husband, and I wanted to make sure you weren't pulled in for questioning without my knowledge."

"Okay." A chill enveloped her despite the intense heat of an Italian summer day. Had her haven become a no-go zone?

"Please allow my man, Pietro, to see you safely to the farm." Batista's voice was calmly reassuring, like he hadn't just told her that her life was potentially in danger.

Bella swallowed. "Have you spoken to Matteo?"

"Yes. I talked to him very early this morning, which must have been late at night in New York."

How did he sound? Was he upset? Did he say anything about me? Not really the questions you could ask a lawyer you'd met only once. She forced herself to think practically. "Do you know if Interpol has been advised of the warrant?" Would Matteo be arrested trying to fly out of New York? Or as he landed in Tunis? At least she knew he wouldn't be crazy enough to follow her here.

"We don't believe so. I'm working as hard as I can to prove him innocent. But until his memory returns or he's able to provide some further evidence as to his actions that day, it's very difficult."

"I understand. Thank you."

The drive to the farm was pleasant enough. Pietro didn't seem the type of man to make small talk so she managed to nap for at least an hour. As they neared the village, he put a hand on her arm and asked for directions to the farm.

The gate was unlocked, and when Pietro stopped in front of the cottage, Bella waited for the peace and tranquility that usually came over her when she returned home. Instead, an aching emptiness filled her.

Angela flew out of the cottage and wrapped Bella in a hug as soon as she stepped from the car. "Oh, who's this?" she asked, when she saw it wasn't Matteo behind the wheel.

"A nice man who gave me a lift from the airport." She'd explain all that had happened later. She ducked her head through the open window. "*Grazie*, Pietro."

"I'll see you around, *Signora*," he replied in Italian. Which meant his job wasn't finished. But he reversed the car and returned up the driveway. Probably to find some vantage point where he could observe without being noticed.

Everything was the same as when she'd left. The donkey and horse were in the field next to the barn. Akbar stared down his nose at her but made no move to come closer to the fence. In the distance, she could hear a few of the ewes bleating and calling to their lambs. The bees buzzed in the lavender and one of the dogs slinked over, hoping for a treat. No one had missed her or was excited to see her return.

"You look like you could use a coffee," Angela said, leading the way to the cottage. "What happened to your luggage?"

"Yes to the coffee. Long story on the luggage. Where's the little girl?"

"Holly is with her parents. Her mother came back this morning, all apologetic and promised she'd care for her daughter. They're going to leave tomorrow morning. Evidently, the husband has agreed to go into treatment. Sorry, looks like I called you away for nothing."

"Not nothing. I needed to come home." Except it no longer felt like home.

"We're happy to stay on here as long as you want," Angela said, a little hopefully, as she prepared a coffee for them.

"What about your café?"

"Well, Tony's cousin and her husband are visiting from Napoli. They can't get work there and were wondering if I could hire them."

In other words, if I leave the farm, I could provide two young couples with jobs and a place to live.

It seemed the farm would be fine without her. Still, Kai's words rang in her ears. *Don't become one of them—a woman without a purpose.*

She swallowed down the coffee like it was the elixir of life and forced a smile for Angela. "I need to be alone for a while to think. I'm going to take a walk down to the cliff." Stare across the sea and imagine Matteo in bed in his Tunisian palace.

"Okay. I'll have some supper ready in about an hour. If you see Tony, can you let him know the special feed for the animals has arrived, but I didn't want to carry it into the barn?" Angela rubbed her belly, tellingly.

"Are you pregnant?"

"Yup, only two months, but we're really excited."

"Congratulations." Bella's period had arrived on schedule yesterday morning, so she knew she wasn't expecting. She just hadn't decided yet if she was relieved or disappointed.

Five minutes later, Bella had changed into jeans and a T-shirt, slipped off her black stilettos, and pulled on her boots. Back in sheep farmer mode.

Tony was in the east paddock when she passed, inspecting the progress on the new stone fence. She congratulated him on his soon-to-be fatherhood and passed on Angela's message about the feed. He hurried off to move it, and Bella wandered over to the cliff's edge. From here, she could see the beach and far out into the changing blue of the Mediterranean.

The couple staying at the guesthouse was lying on the beach; both looked like they were asleep. Bella scanned the sand for the little girl. Her heart plummeted off the cliff when she saw her in a small inflatable boat drifting out of the bay. Seconds from now, the girl would be in the open sea. Bella screamed down to the parents, but they didn't move.

She raced down the path, yelling as she went. A helicopter flew low overhead, but she didn't take the time to see who it was. Maybe it was the coast guard and they had spotted the child in distress as well. By the time she hit the sand, the mother at least was sitting up, looking around, confused.

"Your daughter…" Bella sucked in air all the while pulling off her boots. She gestured toward the water. The mother stood and wobbled, nearly falling onto the dad, who still snored away. A bottle of wine and one of scotch lay on the sand, both empty. Neither parent would be any help rescuing the little girl.

"Go up to the cottage and tell Angela to call

emergency services."

Yanking off her jeans, Bella rushed to the water, praying she'd be in time. Anger added to the adrenaline; she didn't even notice the cold. But one hundred feet from shore, her lungs and muscles burned. Despite all her activities, swimming had never been her forte. When she was about ten feet from the little girl, a strong gust of wind blew the inflatable boat farther away and the child began to cry.

"Hang on, Holly. I'm coming for you. Stay as low as possible in the boat," Bella yelled. A wave hit her face and she swallowed a mouthful of water. Every muscle protested as she swam toward the boat, now at least twenty feet from her and drifting farther out every second. Would she even have the strength to get them both back to land?

"Bella!" She heard her name shouted from shore but didn't have the energy to look back. It sounded too much like Matteo. Another large wave smashed into her and she gasped for air. Was she drowning? She'd heard people had hallucinations before they died.

At least her last thought would be of Matteo.

***

Matteo stripped off his clothes as fast as he could before plunging into the sea. He'd met the frantic mother on her way up to the cottage. All she'd said was her daughter was in trouble and a strange woman had gone into the water after her. He knew it was Bella. As he dove under the cresting wave, his heart rate spiked and the blackness at the back of his mind threatened to take over.

It was the first time he'd been fully submerged in water since he'd awakened in a Tunis hospital with no idea who he was.

He broke the surface and tried to see Bella and the little inflatable boat with the child. His panic attack would have to wait. The wind had picked up, increasing the wave activity. The quickest way was under the water, but then he couldn't keep his destination in sight. Soon the waves were too high to see beyond the next one. He prayed he was headed in the right direction. Screaming Bella's name, he kicked his legs upward, hoping to catch sight of her.

"Matteo!" Her answering call was to the left. He adjusted his angle and soon spotted her frantically bobbing in the water. He reached her just as her head disappeared below the surface. Diving down, he grabbed her by the arm and dragged her above the water again.

"She's too far out, I can't reach her," Bella shouted. Another wave broke over them and she spluttered. Three sleepless nights were taking their toll on him; his strength was waning.

Save his wife or save a child he'd never met? No man should have to make that decision.

"How are you even in here?" Bella asked.

"More scared of losing you than the water," he managed. He focused on her face, forcing the terror to the back of his mind. He had to do this. He couldn't fail. To lose Bella again would kill him.

"Can you save her? One more wave and I'm sure she'll tip." Bella kicked upward and pointed at the small boat where a little hand could be seen clinging to the side. The child's terrified screaming filled his ears. The screams, together with the water, threatened to take him under.

Focus, Matteo!

"I can make it back to shore," Bella said.

"Are you sure?" He could see the exhaustion in her face and her kicks were barely enough to keep her above the water.

"Yes. For our love. For you. I promise."

It was the hardest thing he'd ever done to let her go and kick his legs in the opposite direction. He spotted the small boat as it crested a wave and put all his remaining energy into reaching it. He was less than a meter away when it capsized, flinging the little girl into the water.

His heartbeat pounded in his ears, deafening him to all other sounds as he dove, searching for the tiny body. His lungs burned as he went deeper; the pressure to breathe became intense. His eyesight began to blur as his oxygen-deprived brain began shutting down nonessential functions. Just as he couldn't take the pain any longer, he spotted something pink to his left. He reached out a hand, praying it was the child and not a jellyfish.

When he broke the surface again, he thrust the object up above him. He gulped in air and tried to clear his eyes of the salt water. It was the girl, but she was as lifeless as a doll. He held her as high as possible, but still she didn't breathe. He was not going to risk his wife's life and his own to fail now. Hauling in a lungful of air, he covered the child's mouth and nose with his own and gently blew the air into her body. If her lungs were already full of water, it might not make a difference.

Where had the boat gone? Maybe if he could put her back inside she'd recover. His thigh muscles protested every movement and it was increasingly difficult to keep both their heads above the surface of the water. Another gust of wind flipped the inflatable into the air. Minus the girl's weight, it became airborne. When it next touched down it was too far away to be of any use.

Holding the little body as high as he could, he had only his legs to power them toward the shore. Was this how it was going to end? The sea had taken six years of his marriage, would it now take his life as well?

No! Bella had promised to make it to shore. He would, too.

An image of his wife's smiling face as she won a hand of strip poker flashed through his mind and he focused on that and not the agony of exhausted muscles or the too-still child in his arms. Another wave crashed over them and they both went underwater for a second. As he struggled to surface, the little girl twitched. They both gulped in air as they broke through. *Grazie a Dio*, she lived. Now he had to keep it that way. He flipped over on his back and put the child on his chest and kicked for all he was worth.

Wave after wave splashed over his face. His brain filled with images of clinging to the rubber dock bumper on the side of a boat, his ears still reverberating with the staccato gunfire. Boat? Gunfire? He was back six years ago, to the fishing expedition that had netted him amnesia.

Suddenly, hands pulled the little girl from him and a pair of arms dragged his weary body up onto the land. He collapsed on the beach without even the energy to lift his head from the sand.

A gentle hand that could only be Bella's wiped a strand of hair off his face. Through the pounding of his heartbeat in his ears came the sound of women crying, a man shouting, and distant sirens. He should move. The sirens were danger. He wasn't supposed to be here. But even that knowledge couldn't force his muscles into action.

Someone rolled him over, and then Bella pulled his head and shoulders up so she could cradle him in her arms. She wiped the sand from his cheeks and pressed kisses on his forehead as she murmured over and over how much she loved him. Warmth filled him. His muscles spasmed. Didn't you feel warm just before you died?

"It's okay, *mi amore*. You're safe. And you saved her. Holly is going to live."

The voices got louder as his heart rate calmed, and he opened one eye, then the other. At first all he could see was Bella's beautiful face. Tears coursed down her cheeks and the smile she attempted failed miserably. But she was alive. He was alive. What more could they want?

"I thought I'd lost you so many times. You kept going under..." she sobbed.

He tried to speak but coughed up water instead. And once he started coughing, he couldn't stop. Bella twisted him to his side and he vomited out a stomach-full of sea.

When he opened his eyes again, the beach was crowded with people. A man and woman hovered near the paramedic who tended to the little girl. Tony stood comforting his wife, who cried as if it were her child who'd nearly drowned. Two police officers arrived on the scene and started asking questions.

"Bella, I have to get out of here." His throat was so raw it hurt to talk.

"I know," she whispered against his temple. "Can you walk?"

Could he? Doubtful, but he had to try. Being arrested had not been on his to-do list today. Getting his wife back had.

He sat up and tried to pull his legs under him only to have the muscles cramp. Biting his tongue to stop himself from screaming in pain, he shook his head at Bella.

One of the police officers detached from interviewing the girl's parents and came to stand over him. "Matteo Vanni? You are under arrest for the murders of Stefano Pirlo, Ciro De Rossi, and Leonardo Insigne."

Chapter Seventeen

No way in hell were they taking her husband after he'd just saved a child from drowning. Especially not after she'd realized she couldn't live without him.

"You've got it all wrong, officer," she said, her arms tightening around Matteo. "This is Mario Barilla. There's no Matteo Vanni here."

The officer looked confused and checked his notepad. "That woman over there," he pointed at Angela, "said his name was Matteo Vanni. We just received the arrest warrant for him yesterday."

"Angela is mistaken. She's new to the area. Matteo Vanni was my first husband. I'm filing for divorce so I can marry this man, Mario Barilla. I have the paperwork at the farm if you'd like to see it."

He turned back to Matteo. "Signore, where are your documents?"

Matteo coughed up more of the sea but managed to point at his clothes farther up the beach. The police officer moved to retrieve them, and Bella motioned Angela forward.

"Angela, can you get *Mario* something to drink?" she asked. Bella did her best to convey with her eyes the change in name.

"Of course." Angela hurried off to get a bottle of water from the cooler they kept stocked in a tiny alcove of the cliff. She whispered something to Tony on the way.

The policeman had Matteo's passport in hand and was checking the photo and details. He then flipped through the pages. "When did you arrive in Italy, Signor Barilla?"

"This afternoon," Matteo managed. Angela handed him the water and he drank half of it before lowering the bottle.

"There is no entry stamp in your passport." The officer flipped through the pages again.

Before Matteo could respond, the policeman turned to Angela. "Signora, who is this man?"

"Signora Vanni's friend, Mario. I can't remember his last name," Angela answered. She now spoke Italian with a really bad American accent.

"A minute ago you said his name was Matteo Vanni," the policeman argued.

Angela lifted her shoulders. "I meant to say he is the man friend of Signora Vanni. I get the pronouns and order mixed up sometimes. I was upset at seeing the little girl almost die."

The policeman shook his head, and Bella couldn't tell whether he believed Angela or not. He stared at her for a moment longer, but Angela never looked away. Bella so wanted to hug her friend right now. Tony was called over and asked the same question. He responded as Angela had.

Matteo had recovered enough to stand, and Bella wrapped her arms around his waist to support him.

The policeman held up Matteo's passport. "You have not answered why there is no new immigration stamp in your passport. As a Tunisian citizen, you are required to go through customs and immigration on entering Italy."

"Signora Vanni and I had an argument and she returned to Sicily. In my haste to apologize to her, I hired a helicopter to fly me straight to her farm. I have a valid visitor's visa."

"I can charge you with entering the country illegally," the policeman said.

Bella put herself in between Matteo and the policeman. "Are you really going to arrest a man who just saved a little girl from drowning? Especially as the little girl is a tourist? He should get a medal for his bravery. Imagine what the international media will say when they read this headline: Man trying to reconcile with girlfriend saves little girl only to be arrested by heartless police."

The policeman narrowed his eyes, and for a second her heart stalled, sure she was about to be handcuffed alongside Matteo for insubordination.

"*Sì*, Signora. In light of Signor Barilla's heroism, we will overlook his transgression if he leaves the country immediately." The policeman handed Matteo his passport and then strode over to Holly's parents. The paramedics had loaded her on a stretcher and were preparing to carry her up the hill to where Bella assumed an ambulance waited.

"Thank you," Matteo said, wrapping both arms around her and snuggling her against his chest. God, she'd come so close to losing him again.

She'd find something to do, some way to stay sane in order to keep this man in her life. "You'd better leave before Roberto Della Vedova finds out you're here," she said as everyone else left the beach.

"He's the killer. I remembered everything in the water."

"Then you definitely need to leave."

"I'm not going without you," Matteo said, tightening his hold on her.

"*Amore...*" She was afraid to use his real name now.

"Bella, I lost you once. I refuse to do it again. I'll fight to clear my name, even if it's from a jail cell, if you want to stay on the farm."

He'd give up his freedom for her? She'd never accept that sacrifice. "I can't ask that of you."

He released her enough to stare into her eyes. "Come with me. Please. You are not an accessory to my accomplishments. You are my world. I'm nothing without you. I was terrified that if I told you I might never be able to return to Sicily, it would be the straw that tipped the scales in favor of the camel. I wanted my full two weeks to show you how much I love you. I never meant to shut you out or treat you as anything less than you are, which is amazing. My instinct is to cherish and protect, but if I take it too far and you think I'm princessing you, just kick me in the shin."

The tears started again with no hope of stopping them this time. Pietro, the man who had given her a ride from the airport, came running onto the beach. "There are more police arriving, this time from the regional force. You have to leave now!" he shouted.

Her heart stalled and it was hard to breathe. *Think, Bella.* "You said you arrived by helicopter. Where is it?"

"In the east pasture."

"Can you run?"

"I don't even think I can walk," he admitted.

It was true; in the last couple of minutes he'd leaned more heavily on her. Bella's heart pounded again. Fear, like she'd experienced every time Matteo's head had disappeared under the water, swamped her system with adrenaline. Could they hide? Could she outwit or head off Roberto Della Vedova before he found Matteo?

There was a loud commotion at the top of the beach trail. Bella stepped in front of Matteo, although he was so much larger than her it was a futile attempt to hide him. She squinted, and her knees nearly buckled when she saw Tony arrive with Akbar at full trot, Estella the lovesick chicken running alongside. The camel ran right up to them, and again the dromedary didn't complain when ordered to kneel.

Tony jumped off, handed Bella her passport, and then he helped Matteo mount the animal, with Bella behind. Miraculously, the camel seemed to sense the urgency and took off at a gallop once they were atop. They made it to the waiting helicopter just as the regional police crested the hill.

Della Vedova's shouts were drowned out by the blades of the chopper whirling to life. Bella helped Matteo in and then slapped Akbar's rump and sent him cantering toward the police who scattered at the sight of the large animal bearing down on them, flanked by a crazy chicken.

Bella buckled her seatbelt and gripped Matteo's hand tightly as the helicopter lifted off. Circumstances might have hastened her decision but her heart was fully on board.

As the helicopter flew low over the sea, Matteo wrapped his arm around her shoulder.

The farm disappeared behind them. This time, she didn't look back. Her home, her life was with the man next to her.

This girl knew what to do.

***

Matteo lay back against the pillows. It was a bit embarrassing to have a meeting with law enforcement and his lawyer while lying in bed. But the only way he'd managed to avoid a hospital stay was by promising to rest for at least twenty-four hours. And Bella was adamant that he follow the doctor's orders. When he'd arrived back in the country wearing only his boxers, he'd been taken directly to the hospital to be checked out.

Truth was, every muscle in his body screamed with pain and his lungs still wheezed like they were full of water. He'd do it all again, though, to save the girl and have Bella at his side.

The police officer placed a recording device on the bedside table. "Signor Vanni, this conversation will be recorded and may be used in court."

Batista Preatori nodded. "I have a signed document from the Guardia di Finanza that, in exchange for this testimony, Mario Barilla will not be linked to this statement. We can't rescind the charges against Matteo Vanni without alerting Roberto Della Vedova that he is under investigation. However, as long as you continue to use your assumed name you should be safe from extradition. I still advise you against returning to Italy until this is all resolved."

Matteo glanced over at Bella, who sat on the end of the bed, opposite side to the plainclothes law enforcement official and the lawyer. "What about my wife? Can she return? She has a farm and businesses in Sicily." She'd left it all for him. And despite her reassurances that she didn't regret walking away from everything she'd created, once the shock wore off from yesterday's events, she might feel differently.

"Angela and Tony have agreed to look after things for as long as I want. I don't need to return any time soon," Bella said.

"I have a suggestion in that regard," Batista said. "But first, let's get your statement down so the inspector can be on his way."

The police officer pressed play on the machine and asked each of them to state their name and nationality for the record. He then administered an oath to Matteo, requiring him to tell the truth on penalty of prosecution. "*Bene*. Now, Signor Vanni, please recount exactly what occurred on the day you disappeared."

"I went down to the docks to barter for some fish. When I arrived, most of the boats were out, but one, the *Naiadi,* was still in port. Stefano Pirlo, Ciro De Rossi, and Leonardo Insigne were on deck. I knew all three from school. I asked if they had any fish for sale, and they replied they were just heading out. It did seem odd to me because most of the boats went out early and returned about that time, but I knew very little about fishing so didn't question them. I remember thinking, however, that if I went with them and helped on the boat, they might give me a fish or two for free. I had no money at the time." He glanced over at Bella. Did she still feel guilty for asking him for a change in their diet?

"They huddled together for a minute," he continued, "and I thought they were about to refuse. I said I was strong and could help, so they agreed that I could go with them. We set out around 3:00 p.m. and went south at high speed. After about an hour, I asked when we were going to put down the nets and they just laughed. I was annoyed because I'd hoped to be back by suppertime and now that didn't look likely."

He started to cough and Bella handed him a glass of water. It was remembering his stupidity that clogged his throat.

"Eventually, about two hours after we left port we slowed down. We couldn't have been far from the Tunisian coast, as I could see land on the horizon. Again I asked about lowering the nets, and Stefano handed me a fishing rod, pointed to the bait box, and told me to 'knock myself out.' I already knew I was in trouble, that this was not a fishing trip, before the sound of another boat reached my ears." He paused, letting the memory settle.

"Can you describe this other vessel? Where did it come from? Who was aboard?" the inspector asked.

"It was a large inflatable with three men on board,

all armed with machine guns. In the middle were about ten wooden crates."

"Did you recognize any of the men?"

"No, they all wore masks, and by that point I knew I was in deep shit and didn't want to draw any attention to myself. In fact, I hid in the cabin the entire time they transferred the cargo to the fishing boat." A trickle of perspiration edged down his spine as he relived the moment when he'd heard the outboard motor start again and he didn't have a bullet in him. He'd finally been able to breathe. If he'd known that was to be the least of his problems, he would have jumped overboard right then.

"Did they say anything? Think hard." The inspector leaned closer, his eyes searching Matteo's. "Would you be able to recognize the voices?"

"No. No one said much and even that was spoken in a whisper. I think all parties knew what they were there for. It seemed to me it wasn't the first time they'd done this."

The inspector nodded. "How long did the exchange take?"

"Less than ten minutes. After the inflatable left, Ciro turned the boat back toward Sicily and gunned the engine."

"The Tunisian Coast Guard never approached? Or any aircraft fly low overhead?"

"No. As I learned after waking up in a hospital in Tunis, the country was in the midst of the Arab Spring uprising. An aircraft carrier probably could have docked a hundred meters offshore and they wouldn't have had the manpower to investigate."

The inspector nodded. "How far did you travel back toward Italy?"

"About halfway then another boat approached. This one was fiberglass, about seven meters long and it had a light rack above the wheel and official-looking insignia. I could tell from the body language of the other men that this was bad news. They talked about throwing the cargo overboard, but before they could do it the boat was nearly alongside. That's when Leonardo said, 'It's okay, it's Roberto. Stop the boat.'"

"What did you do?"

"Aside from crap my pants? I moved to the far side of the boat. As the other vessel approached, I could see two men in uniform aboard. One was Roberto Della Vedova, the other I don't know."

"And how did Stefano, Ciro, and Leonardo react to this new arrival? Did they seem nervous?"

"They were a bit confused. They kept asking each other if the exchange was going to take place here and weren't they supposed to take the cargo to the regular drop point? No matter what was going down, I knew I was in the wrong place at the wrong time with the wrong people. Either the men on the other boat were real cops and I was about to be arrested for smuggling, or they were in on the deal and I was going to be eliminated because I knew too much. The best I could hope for was that I'd be blackmailed into joining their crew." He closed his eyes for a second. The overwhelming sense of failing Bella and his father flooded his system once again, taking his breath.

Bella moved to sit beside him and ran her hand up and down his arm. He took a moment to stare into her eyes, which were awash with tears. He'd thought that day that he'd never see her again. Even with her inches from him, the same sinking desperation filled him. "I love you," she whispered in English, faint enough that the recording device would be hard pressed to pick it up. Peace washed over him as his heart swelled with love. He prayed this utter contentment never ended.

"What happened?" The inspector's impatient voice brought him back to the present.

"I slipped over the side of the boat near the front and held onto the rubber dock bumper hanging on the side. From the reflection in the glass window I could see what was happening on the rear deck. The two boats were tied together and Roberto told the others to transfer the cargo to his boat. When Ciro questioned him on the change in plans, he said, 'I'm the boss. Just do as I say.' They moved it all onto the police boat. As they were lifting the last box, I heard Leonardo comment that maybe they'd been discovered and Roberto was taking the load so he could claim he'd confiscated it."

The inspector made a few notes on a piece of paper then motioned for Matteo to continue. "To confirm, all the cargo was loaded onto Roberto Della Vedova's boat?"

"Yes."

"How did the three men die?"

Matteo swallowed. Even six years later the memory sickened him. "Roberto Della Vedova took the automatic rifle from the man with him and shot them in the head."

"Roberto Della Vedova himself killed them?" At

227

Matteo's nod, the inspector continued, "And you will testify to that in court? You could clearly see this from the side of the boat?"

Matteo glanced at Bella. If Della Vedova was part of the Cosa Nostra crime group, testifying would be risky. While it could clear the Vanni name, it might never be safe for him, or Bella, to return to Italy. "The mirror in the cabin reflected on the window above my head. I know what I saw. As for testifying, at this point it would be my word against his and he's an officer of the law. If you had other evidence…"

"We're working on it," Batista said. "Did anyone say anything about what type of cargo it was or where it was going or coming from?"

"It was guns. Ciro popped open a crate and inspected one, showing the others. I don't know where they were coming from, and all they said about destination was the cove near Sovareto."

The inspector nodded. "When the other men were shot by Della Vedova how did you survive?" Was there a hint of suspicion in the inspector's voice?

"The man with Della Vedova threw Stefano, Ciro, and Leonardo's bodies overboard. Then he was told to put the boat's engines on full, heading back south. The man asked how he was supposed to get off and Della Vedova said to jump overboard and he'd pick him up. When he went into the cabin, I tried to get the dock bumper unhooked, knowing I was about to be dragged at high speed, but I only managed to get one rope free."

"Did this other man make it off the boat?"

"I have no idea. As soon as the boat started to move, I concentrated all my energy on hanging on. I couldn't see anything because of the spray. I could barely even breathe, and I was continually smashing against the side of the boat. That must be how I was concussed and lost my memory. Eventually, the other line holding the bumper snapped and I was free of the boat but adrift in the sea. Della Vedova's boat was nowhere to be seen. The next thing I knew, I woke in a Tunis hospital."

The inspector wrote down a few more notes then stared hard at Matteo. "Anything else?"

He shook his head and sucked in a quick breath at the piercing pain. Talking so long had given him a massive headache and his chest felt heavy. A bead of sweat trickled down his temple despite the air conditioning.

"That's enough," Bella said, standing. "My husband needs to rest."

"Sì, we're done." The inspector picked up the recording device and stood.

"I need a brief word with my client," Batista said, also standing.

Bella shot him a look and he took a step back.

"Two minutes, I promise," the lawyer said, holding up his hands in a defensive gesture.

She gave him the stink eye but turned toward the inspector. "There are some refreshments ready downstairs. We can wait for Signor Preatori in the courtyard." She glanced pointedly at her watch. "Two minutes."

His overprotective wife left with the police officer, and Matteo closed his eyes for a second. *Dio*, he was tired.

Alexia Adams

But soon Bella would return and all he'd feel was loved. He just hoped she answered yes to the two most important questions he had to ask.

***

Bella slipped into the bedroom. Surely, Matteo must have fallen asleep by now. Batista had appeared downstairs within the allotted two minutes, but she'd stayed to have a cold drink with both men before seeing them out the door.

"*Bellissima*, come lie next to me," Matteo said, his voice husky—whether with exhaustion or desire, she wasn't going to guess. Probably a bit of both.

She searched his face for sign of fever. The doctor had warned that with the amount of salt water he'd had in his lungs, they needed to watch for infection. "You should be sleeping. I noticed you rubbing your temples earlier. Do you want your headache pills?"

"In a minute. First I want to hold you."

The reassurance of his arms around her was exactly what she needed as well. She'd woken several times with nightmares of him disappearing beneath the waves and never surfacing. Her heart had stalled until she nestled against his chest and heard his beating solidly against her ear.

She snuggled next to him, careful not to knock his legs, which he'd told her earlier still throbbed with muscle spasms. "What did Batista have to say?"

Matteo paused, and she held her breath. What could be worse than being wanted by both the police and the mafia? "He warned me there's a possibility I

230

may never have my name cleared. I may never be able to return to Italy," he said.

She sat up so she could see his face and gently caressed his cheek. "I'm sorry, Matteo. It must be dreadful to think you can never go to your homeland."

"You are my home, Bella. If I'm with you, I have no need for any other place."

He pulled her head down for a kiss so full of love she had to blink back the moisture in her eyes. She'd love this man till the day she died. And quite possibly beyond.

"Does that mean I can't go back to Sicily either? I'm okay with giving up the day-to-day running of the farm, but I'd like to think that one day our children will at least be able to visit their heritage."

"Our children? Are you..." The excitement that lit his eyes was so bright she hated to dim it.

"No. Not yet. But I don't want to waste any more time. Let's have a baby, Matteo."

"I'd like that, too. First though, Batista suggests you officially divorce Matteo Vanni and wed Mario Barilla. That way, you'll be able to reenter Sicily and check on the farm whenever you need to."

She cocked her head to one side while she considered the plan. "One problem. I don't recall Mario Barilla asking me to marry him. Do I have to run him off the road as well?"

"Ha! So you finally admit the accident was your fault." A full-blown smile lifted Matteo's lips.

Bella ran her hands up his chest and down his arms until their fingers laced together.

"The recording device is gone, and I don't recall

admitting anything of the sort," she replied.

He rubbed the back of her hand across his cheek, rough from a day's stubble. "Let's skip the car-tractor crash this time and claim the escape on a camel as our story." He let go of her hand and reached over to pull a small box out of the bedside drawer. "Excuse me if I don't get down on one knee. I'm not sure I can get up again." He raised her left hand and kissed her ring finger. "Bella Maria Vanni, will you marry me?" He removed a ring from the box and slid it onto the appropriate finger.

She had to blink away the tears. "My ring. I mean the Vanni ring. How did you get it back?"

"Nothing's impossible if you want it badly enough. And I want you, Bella, as my wife, forever."

There was no stopping the tears now. It was only a piece of metal and stone, but it meant so much more. "You have me. Always. Forever." She punctuated each word with a heartfelt kiss. No matter what happened, they'd make it work.

"I'll take that as a yes."

"That's a hell yes." She moved in to kiss him but stopped inches from his lips. "Can I still call you Matteo when we make love?"

"*Tesori*, when we make love, you can call me anything you want."

Their lips joined and soon she had trouble remembering her own name. As Matteo dragged in a breath he wheezed, and she pulled away. She was supposed to be nursing him back to health, not leading him to an early—albeit with a smile on his face— grave.

As she snuggled next to him, Matteo wrapped his arms around her. "I know you like to be busy," he said, his lips against her forehead, "so in addition to being Signora Barilla and the mother of my children, I'm hoping you'll also be the education director for the charity that oversees the improvements to the villages we work with. It will be your responsibility to decide when the schools are built and hire the staff, etc."

"Really?" That set off the waterworks again. She was so happy she could barely speak.

"Bella, talk to me. If it's not something you want to do..." The anguish in his voice stung.

She sat up. "It's everything I want to do. Travel with you, be at your side, help those children. It's an amazing opportunity. Thank you."

He wiped a tear from her cheek. Playful Matteo was back in his eyes. "You do realize, however, that I will be your boss and you'll have to do as I say?"

Her laugh ended on a hiccup. "Oh, *amore*. You know that's not how it's going to work."

"Yes, but it was worth a shot." His gorgeous smile released one of her own.

"Keep dreaming, Matteo."

"With you in my arms, I already am."

****

Thank you for reading *The Sicilian's Forgotten Wife*. Please post a review where you purchased the book. Your opinion will not only help other readers decide whether to buy the book or not, it will also help me continue to write the stories that I, and hopefully you, love to read. Thank you!

Have you read my Love in Translation series?

Thailand with the Tycoon

A reluctant traveler. A stunning translator. Will being trapped in a failing resort change more than their itinerary?

Caleb Doyle checked out of the family hotel business years ago to follow his own path—ending up with piles of money, a jam-packed schedule, and a burning desire to scale cliff faces to escape the tedium of it all. When his older brother suffers a heart-attack, Caleb is sucked back into the family's virtually bankrupt business. He reluctantly travels to Thailand to evaluate a last-chance resort with the help of a translator. Getting stranded with an enchanting local was not on the agenda. Neither was discovering a new purpose in life.

Malee Wattana has returned to northeastern Thailand to help her grandparents as they recover from various health difficulties. For the past thirteen years

235

she's dreamed of having her family back together. If she can convince the wealthy hotelier to buy the nearby resort property, it will bring much needed employment to the area and allow her mother to return. But getting stranded with her sexy boss soon has her questioning everything she thought she wanted from life. Until an unexpected revelation forces her to choose between her family and love.

Can Caleb and Malee overcome their baggage to claim a suite at love's best hotel?

Thailand with the Tycoon is a light-hearted contemporary romance. If you enjoy funny and romantic stories with family dramas and happily-ever-afters, then you'll love this delightful tropical tale.

Thailand with the Tycoon

Chapter One

Caleb ran his fingers along the rock face, searching for a hold. He dislodged a pebble and it bounced down the cliff until he couldn't hear it anymore. That meant he was near the top … and a fall now would definitely kill him. God, he was exhausted. Why the hell had he started his ascent this late in the day? If he wasn't off the mountain soon, he'd either have to risk the climb in the dark or cling where he was until dawn.

But after the week he'd had, the need to escape the office and breathe fresh, clean, non-profit-oriented air had led him to his current situation. Starting his own venture capital firm—getting in at the start of some amazing businesses and ideas—had sounded like fun. But it had quickly morphed into constant meetings and investment reports. At least falling 700 meters down the Stawamus Chief would be a better death than his father's: having a heart attack Friday night and being found Monday morning on the boardroom floor. No one had missed him for an entire weekend, because he'd practically lived at the office.

But Caleb wasn't ready to die just yet. There were a lot of things—a lot of women—he still wanted to do.

His fingers found a good hold, and he hauled his sorry ass another few centimeters closer to the summit. An eagle soared overhead as if mocking his puny efforts. Dangling on a granite dome was a damn sight more invigorating than reading about the next great investment, but it wasn't how he wanted to spend his night. He pushed through his tiredness and concentrated on one hold after another until he crested the top, too exhausted to celebrate. Lying on his back, he waited for his heart rate to return to normal while the coldness of the stone seeped into his burning muscles. He rolled to his side and stared at the blue-green water of Howe Sound. He'd lived on the west coast of Canada all his life and traveled around the globe more times than he could count, but this sight always took his breath away. The pristine coastal mountains in the background hinted at adventure. And freedom.

Something kicked at his foot and Caleb turned warily, hoping it wasn't a black bear trying to determine if he was edible. But unless the local wildlife had invaded an Italian shoe store, it was a human standing over him. And considering the inappropriate shoes, expensive suit, and silk tie still tightly fastened at the neck, it could only be one person: Harrison Mackenzie.

"Come to make sure I survived?" Caleb asked, pushing himself into a sitting position.

"When I didn't see your broken body at the base of the Chief, I assumed you'd made it," Harrison said, his voice as always carefully neutral. You never knew if he was excited or depressed. It made him a fabulous lawyer but an annoying friend.

"Great to know you were worried. What's up?" Harrison and nature did not go together, as evidenced by his attire.

Harrison's hands clenched tightly at his sides, providing the only sign something was wrong.

"You need to come back to Vancouver. I've had them reopen the Sea to Sky gondola. The helicopter is waiting in the parking lot." Harrison turned as though expecting Caleb to obediently follow.

"Why?" Caleb stayed where he was, partly because his muscles weren't ready to comply with his brain's demand to move, but mostly because he hated being told what to do. That's why he'd left the family business to his brother and branched out on his own. Unfortunately, he then became wildly successful, creating his own leg-hold trap of board meetings, contract negotiations, and endless investment reports. He should have opened a rock-climbing school or one of those ninja warrior gyms. Maybe that would be his next challenge: to finally do something he was passionate about. Perhaps it would soothe the itch inside that pushed him to take ever-greater risks.

"I'll tell you on the way." Harrison's leather-soled shoes slipped on the smooth granite, and instinctively Caleb leapt to his feet to stop his friend from falling. Great lawyers were replaceable, but ones who put up with Caleb's shit and took his calls at three in the morning were a little rarer.

"We need to hurry," Harrison said, once he'd

regained his footing.

Caleb crossed his arms, ignoring the protest of his muscles. "Unless you tell me why it's so urgent I go back to Vancouver, I'm heading to Whistler for the weekend." He narrowed his eyes. "If this is my mother's latest way to summon me, you'd better start looking for a new job on Monday."

He had a vague recollection of his admin assistant reminding him that his mother was back in town and expected him to pay her a visit. But he'd spent enough years dancing attendance on that woman. He was done playing her games. Besides, her lame attempts at pretending she cared were always simply a prelude to a request for money. She'd already gone through what his father had left to her. And with his brother's company failing, she'd turned to Caleb to maintain her lavish lifestyle. In short, she expected him to pay her damn bills, even though she hadn't called him once on his birthday since he'd left home at eighteen.

Harrison kept walking, not even turning around to answer. "I know better than to get between you and your mother. It's Ian. Your brother has had a heart attack. And he won't settle until he speaks with you."

"Shit." Ian was only eight years older than Caleb. Forty was way too early to have heart problems. At least Patrick, their dad, had made it to fifty before he fell apart.

Caleb followed Harrison down the path toward the gondola. Far below, he could see a helicopter in the overflow parking lot that wasn't used this late in the season.

"Is Ian going to be okay?" There were enough

years between them that they'd never been close as brothers. Ian had insisted that Caleb was making a huge mistake when he left the family hotel business to start his own ventures. His doubts had been a massive incentive for Caleb to prove his brother wrong by out-earning him.

Once that had been accomplished, the tension between them had notched up another degree. Now, they only saw each other three times a year: at Mother's birthday party, the Doyle Destinations AGM—Caleb still held a minority share—and at the major fundraiser for the charity their mother had set up in memory of Patrick Doyle. Not that Claire wanted to memorialize a man who had been a shadow in all their lives. She simply liked being the center of attention, and this was her way to get it.

"They were still running tests when I left," Harrison replied as they got in the gondola for the quick ride down the mountain. "His secretary found him slumped over his desk and called 911."

"Who called you?"

"Your sister-in-law. Evidently, as soon as Ian regained consciousness, he started asking for you and became agitated. When you didn't answer your phone, Sarah called me and requested I hunt you down."

"My phone is locked in my car," Caleb said. The gondola doors opened, and a cool breeze off the ocean swept over them. The warmth and adrenaline from his climb had worn off, leaving him chilled. He was going to hurt like a bitch tomorrow.

Harrison shouted as the helicopter blades started to turn. "I'll drive your car back and leave the keys in your condo."

Caleb handed over his car keys and ran for the open helicopter door. He'd barely got his seatbelt buckled before it lifted off for the flight back to the city.

***

The rubber soles of his rock-climbing shoes squeaked on the polished tile floor of St. Paul's Hospital. The sterile air was a sharp contrast to the pure mountain freshness he'd been breathing half an hour ago.

The woman at the information desk did a double-take when she glanced up from her computer. "The emergency department is down that hall," she said, pointing to her left.

He quirked an eyebrow at her reply then followed her gaze down his body. He hadn't taken the time to change out of his skin-tight climbing gear, and his arms and legs were covered with the myriad scratches he'd gotten rubbing intimately against Mother Nature. He looked like he'd been dragged behind a bus for half a block.

"I'm fine. I'm here to see my brother, Ian Doyle. Has he been transferred to a ward yet? I was told he had a heart attack earlier today."

"Oh, sorry." Her eyes made one more appreciative pass over his body before returning to her computer. "Ian Doyle is in the cardiac unit, room 710." She gave him directions to the ward then flashed another smile. "I'll be here until eight if there's anything else I can help with." Her gaze locked on his. "Anything at all."

He gave her a smile and a wink to make her day before striding down the hall. If there was one thing he'd learned, it was that nice, normal girls spelled trouble. Like, "wanting a relationship" trouble. It was far better to stick to shallow women who were only interested in a good time. Because that was all he had to offer.

He paused outside the designated room, getting his game face ready. His brother's agitated voice, as well as his sister-in-law's calming one, floated through the thin walls.

"Hey, who said you could take a holiday?" Caleb said in the cheeriest tone he could manage. He wrapped an arm around his sister-in-law, Sarah, to give her some support. His mother sat in a chair the other side of the bed, doing something on her phone. She didn't even glance up at the arrival of her youngest child.

"Caleb." Ian's pale face relaxed a fraction, and the heart monitor showed a decrease in his pulse rate. "You have to go to Thailand for me."

That wasn't the request he'd expected. Caleb turned questioning eyes on the petite woman next to him. His twin five-year-old niece and nephew were absent, probably with one of Sarah's family. They were far too young to be without a dad. Caleb would do anything for them.

"Ian was supposed to leave for Thailand tomorrow to finalize negotiations for a new hotel," his sister-in-law said, her voice quavering. There was a desperate fear in her brown eyes. "But as you can see, he can't go."

Caleb took in the beeping monitors that counted

243

his brother's heartbeat, blood pressure, oxygen levels, and other functions the healthy took for granted.

He tightened his arm around Sarah. He'd always liked her; she was the opposite of his mother. Her quiet strength and no-nonsense approach suited Ian completely. How his brother had convinced such a lovely woman to join their frigid family, he had no idea.

"Surely that can wait until you're better," Caleb replied. It was no secret that the hotel business his father had started in the early eighties was facing extinction. People expected something different from their travel experience now, and Doyle Destinations hadn't kept up with the times. It wasn't Ian's fault that their father had so meticulously groomed his eldest son to follow his lead that he'd forgotten how to think independently.

"No, it has to be now. There's another bidder. We have to buy it within the next week. This is the best chance I've got to turn the company around. Without this resort, we'll go bankrupt in eighteen months." Ian's heart rate accelerated while he talked, and his face turned even whiter.

"Please, Caleb." Sarah's soft plea stabbed him right in his ice-shrouded heart and did more to convince him than his brother's recitation. Damsels in distress were his weakness. He could never resist playing the hero. But one more property wasn't going to turn Ian's company around. The whole enterprise needed a major overhaul.

He turned back to his brother. "All right. I'll go. But you promise to get better and be out of here by the time I get back." He gripped Ian's hand where it fidgeted on the bedsheet and gave it a slight squeeze. The differences in their ages and temperaments meant they'd never been close. And given the arctic vortex they'd grown up in, a hand squeeze was about all either of them was comfortable with.

The icy wind that was their mother chose that moment to look up from her phone. In Claire Doyle's mind, the world revolved around her.

"Before you leave, Caleb dear, I need to have word with you about my finances." Trust his mother to discuss money at his brother's hospital bedside. A smile from her would have shocked Caleb into his own heart attack. There were a lot of things you could change in life; Mother wasn't one of them.

"Talk to my accountant," he replied. "I need to go pack."

It really wasn't the time to go gallivanting off to the other side of the globe, but at least this trip to Thailand would warm him up after the chill of being in the same room as his mother. A few quiet days of pampering in a luxury Thai resort while he negotiated on his brother's behalf would be his reward for having to run two companies until Ian was back on his feet again.

And here he'd thought falling down a 700-meter cliff was all he'd have to worry about today.

***

Malee dug her fingernails into the dashboard of her cousin's open-top Jeep. So far, the day had been a complete disaster. This was her first job in three months, and she was on the verge of losing it before she'd even started. The early bus she'd intended to take into the city had been full. Then she'd had to beg her cousin Bodin, her least favorite relative but the only one with a vehicle, to drive her to Nan. Instead of being cooled by the bus's air conditioner, she was being buffeted with hot, humid air. Monsoon season was never pleasant. Coupled with inner turmoil and a dash of sheer panic, Malee was on the verge of a meltdown. Possibly literally.

To top off her day from hell, the pharmacy where they'd stopped to collect her grandmother's prescription had been out of the antibiotic. Phoning around to find the drug had eaten up another precious hour.

She should have let Bodin collect the medicine after he dropped her off at the airport, but he'd been so distracted that she had to remind him three times on the drive from their remote village to stop at the drugstore. He'd always played the village idiot, but he seemed to have ascended to the king of fools' throne recently. Still, he was a close relation. And you had to respect relatives, no matter their IQ. Family was the center around which life revolved.

And the nucleus of Malee's life was her maternal grandparents. *Yai*, her grandmother, had been battling pneumonia for three months now, and if she didn't complete this course of antibiotics, she could end up back in hospital, or worse. A tremor swept through Malee, and she clutched the dash tighter.

Bodin took another corner too fast, and she

clenched her eyes shut to avoid seeing the inevitable collision. The memory of another car crash flitted through her mind. What she wouldn't give to forget…

"Malee, about this job… Don't screw it up." Bodin took his eyes off the road to stare at her and narrowly missed a minivan with a flat tire at the side of the road. At least her horrified gasp at the near-miss gave her time to formulate an appropriate reply. He'd already inferred six times in the past two hours that she couldn't cope with a simple translation assignment. *I'm not the stupid one here, Bodin.*

"I am qualified, cousin." She put as much deference into her tone as possible. Thai custom dictated that she be respectful of her older relative, even if he was being a condescending jerk. Since her grandfather's accident, Bodin had become the de facto head of the family, a position that commanded deference even if the incumbent didn't.

But thirteen years in the Western world had dulled that instinct in Malee. She forced a smile. "If there's one thing I can do, it's speak both Thai and English fluently." She'd lived in London with her mother from the age of twelve.

It was a simple enough assignment. She was to collect Ian Doyle and translate for him in his negotiations to buy the run-down resort near where her grandparents lived in northeastern Thailand. The original owners had never made a success of the place, so she had no idea why this Canadian figured he could do better. Most tourists to Thailand expected pretty beaches and wild nightlife, not dense jungle, masses of mosquitoes, and minimal electricity after dark.

The only visitors to this part of the country were backpackers seeking the "real" Thailand. Like the country had to stay in the seventeenth century to be authentic.

Well, you didn't get much more "real" than unemployed. And if she didn't arrive at the airport in ten minutes, that would remain her reality.

It was more than just her job on the line. If this Canadian hotelier bought the resort and fixed it up, it would provide much-needed work for the little village where most of her relatives still lived. Maybe Malee's mother could come home from London at last. The whole family could be together after fifteen years apart. A flicker of hope overrode the terror of her cousin's driving for an all-too-brief second.

"You sure you don't want me to wait? I can drive you both back to Pakang Yao," Bodin said as he screeched to a halt in front of the arrivals terminal at Nan Nakhon Airport.

Letting her reckless cousin drive her new boss would undoubtedly result in instant dismissal. "It's okay. I'm told he has his transport organized."

Bodin cut the engine and put his hand on her arm, stopping her from getting out. "Malee, about the resort. You know it would mean a lot to the village if it was reopened. You have to convince this foreigner to buy it."

"I'm just assigned to translate."

"You can do more than that. A pretty girl like you, I'm sure you can be persuasive if you want."

Bodin, you are an arse. First you doubt I can speak English well enough, and now you want me to flirt to get a farang *to buy a pile of junk that no reasonable Thai person would take two looks at?*

She lowered her head so he couldn't read the anger blazing in her eyes and cheeks. "The info I received from the translation agency said he's married with two children."

Bodin frowned and kept hold of her. "I'm not asking you to disgrace the family. Just show him the potential of the place. Come on, cousin. Do it for the villagers. Think of all the jobs you'll bring back so the young people don't leave for the city."

Like she needed more stress to add to her already churning stomach. Bodin wasn't the first to bring it up. Word had already spread about the potential sale. The village's fate rested on her shoulders. "I'll try. But I'm not sure how much I can do." She climbed out of the vehicle before her cousin could launch into a lecture.

"Make it happen, Malee." With those parting words, he restarted the Jeep, slammed it back into first gear, and sped off to the blaring of horns from the cars he cut off.

Malee tucked her bag with her change of clothes under her arm and strode toward the airport doors. Bodin's vehicle was never clean, and she hadn't wanted to dirty her dress before she arrived. *Please, let one thing go right today and give me enough time to change.* Mr. Doyle was coming by private jet, and she'd only been given an approximate time of arrival.

The automatic doors opened as she approached, and a very tall, blond man strode out, looking like he'd come to claim Thailand for his own. Everything about the man shrieked conqueror. His pale hair glinted in the sunshine, showing hints of red. A strong jaw and full lips next grabbed her attention. His eyes were hidden behind mirrored aviator sunglasses, but based on his coloring, they were probably either blue or green.

A good Thai woman would lower her gaze and shuffle past without ogling. Malee wasn't a typical Thai woman. She wanted to examine every inch of him. The cultural war within her was damned difficult.

About to move around him as he stood staring at the passing traffic, she stopped abruptly. He wasn't dressed in shorts and sandals. Not even a T-shirt. Instead he wore a full suit and tie that emphasized his broad chest and lean physique. It couldn't be…

"Mr. Doyle?" she asked, praying she was mistaken. This hunk of manhood would make even a proper Thai woman forget about appropriate conduct. A quick glance at his left hand, clutching a briefcase, showed no sign of a wedding band. Was he one of *those* men who took it off when he traveled? The thought alone was enough to turn her stomach. "Sorry, I must be mistaken."

"I'm Doyle," he said. Damn if his voice wasn't dark molten chocolate. "You're not by chance Ms. Wattana?" He removed his sunglasses as his gaze slid over her. The interest in his green eyes was quickly replaced by cool detachment. Had she imagined it? Unfortunately, it didn't stop a shiver of awareness from sweeping through her.

She didn't dare glance at the reflective glass of the airport building to see what she looked like. She could only imagine that her hair was tangled around her head in great clumps, since she'd been holding onto the dashboard too desperately to secure it. She could taste the dust on her lips, feel a trickle of perspiration pool in her bra. This was not the picture of professionalism she'd intended to present. And here he was, having come off an international flight, looking immaculate and sexier than any married man had a right to be.

She put her palms together and bent forward in the customary Thai greeting. "*Sawatdee-kah*. Yes, I'm Malee. I apologize for my clothing. I'd intended to change before you arrived." Her shorts were a couple of years old and faded in the backside, her T-shirt declared Westlife as the best boy band ever, and her sandals had seen better days as well. She'd planned to throw the whole lot in the rubbish after she'd changed.

Mr. Doyle's eyes swept over her again, leaving a trail of tingles in their wake. He gestured at his own outfit. "You're dressed more appropriately than me. It must be forty degrees Celsius. I'm going to melt if I stay in this suit much longer."

"It will be cooler once we get into the mountains. The information package I received said you already had transportation arranged to the resort location." She forced her eyes from the column of tanned skin that appeared as he loosened his tie and undid the top three buttons of his shirt.

Puzzlement flicked in his gaze. "Do I? I skipped over all the technicalities about how to get there as I concentrated on the hotel specifications." He pulled out his phone and began searching.

Malee tilted her head. From the details she'd been provided, Ian Doyle had been in discussions about the property for several months now. Her job was simply to translate as required and ensure there were no items being discussed that he didn't understand.

"There it is. I'm to be met by you here and then we are to proceed to the car rental desk, where a vehicle has been reserved. Do you drive, Malee?"

He turned those amazing green eyes on her once more. "Yes, I drive, but not very well." Certainly not on mountain roads ruled by huge buses and transport trucks and littered with pedestrians, farm animals, wildlife, and hitchhiking tourists willing to risk their lives to save a few baht. And definitely not with this definition of distraction sitting next to her.

"That's fine. I can drive if you can navigate." He reentered the terminal building, and Malee followed behind. Maybe she should call Bodin and get him to drive them to the resort. But subjecting Mr. Doyle to her cousin's death-defying driving style seemed a bit extreme.

At the rental desk, he smiled at the woman behind the counter. A flush crept up the attendant's face and her eyes took on a dazed quality. God, was Malee wearing the same stupid expression? The rental car woman shot a look at Malee and seemed to dismiss her as competition. "How can I help you, sir?"

"You have a car reserved in my brother's name. Ian Doyle. I—"

"Your brother?" Malee blurted out. "So you're not married?"

~~~~~~~~~~

Get your copy of Thailand with the Tycoon now!

252

Thank you, reader

I hope you enjoyed reading Matteo and Bella's story as much as I enjoyed writing it. If you did, **please, please** help others find it by leaving a **review** at your favorite retailer. Your review doesn't have to be long, but your opinion matters to me and other readers.

Want to be one of the first to know about upcoming releases, contests, and events? Sign up for my monthly newsletter at https://alexia-adams.com.

You can also chat with me on Facebook (https://www.facebook.com/AlexiaAdamsAuthor) and Twitter (@AlexiaAdamsAuth) or, of course, get in touch with me via my website (https://alexia-adams.com).

I love to hear from readers, so don't be shy.

And ... if you are wondering about the dedication to Benedict Cumberbatch, here's the story:

One night I was watching BBC's *Sherlock,* you know, the episode when Sherlock comes back from an alleged death and he teases John Watson by pretending to be a waiter. That got me thinking... How would a woman react if her supposedly dead husband just knocked on her door after being gone for six years? *The Sicilian's Forgotten Wife* was born. So, thank you Benedict. (And I'm not sure he knows why, but if he read this, then he would.)

Other Books by Alexia

Love in Translation series:

Thailand with the Tycoon

Caleb reluctantly travels to Thailand to evaluate a last-chance resort that could save his brother's virtually bankrupt hotel business. However, being stranded with an enchanting local wasn't on the itinerary... Malee yearns to reunite her family and getting the local resort open would make that a lot easier. All she has to do is convince the handsome Canadian investor that the derelict property has potential. With secrets and surprises all around them, can Caleb and Malee overcome their baggage to claim a suite at love's best hotel?

Bali with the Billionaire

She's protecting her heart. He's numbing his pain. Will a tropical fling change their future forever? Over a decade since the death of his high school sweetheart and their infant, Harrison Mackenzie has locked his passion away to focus on work. But when a captivating woman without boundaries crashes through the billionaire's broken heart, he wonders if he's worth a second chance after all... Struggling with intense emotions, Harrison and Jade try to keep things strictly physical until a shocking revelation forces the past and the present to collide.

Vintage Love series:

The Vintner and The Vixen

After witnessing a murder, Maya Tessier needs to disappear. So she escapes to the cottage in France she inherited from her great-grandmother where she hopes to start a new life and concentrate on her art. Jacques de Launay doesn't like strangers on his estate, especially when they're a sexy redhead who reminds him of all he's lost. But if he lets her stay, more than his heart may be at risk.

The Playboy and The Single Mum

Single mother Lexy Camparelli must accompany super sexy Formula 1 driver Daniel Michaud for the rest of the race season as part of her job. Will she be able to keep her life on track and her heart from crashing or will the stress of living in the spotlight bring back her eating disorder or worse, jeopardize custody of her son?

The Tycoon and The Teacher

Argentinian tycoon Santiago Alvarez will do whatever it takes to keep custody of his niece Miranda—even if it means marriage to the woman who jeopardizes his peace of mind. Genevieve Dubois is finding her way again after a traumatic experience left her unable to teach in a classroom. Helping an eight-year-old girl come to terms with the loss of her parents is challenge enough without the continual distracting presence of the sexy uncle who refuses to love. Then she discovers the real reason Santiago wants to retain guardianship of Miranda and it threatens all their futures.

The Developer and The Diva

Para siempre means forever. That's what they'd promised one another. Then she left. Now she's back, and para siempre is just two words written on the wall of the community center he's determined to tear down … and she wants to save. Will the pain of the past be too much to overcome, or will they gamble again on a love to last para siempre?

Guide to Love series:

Miss Guided

Mystery writer Marcus Sullivan is determined find someone for his younger brother Liam. Playing matchmaker on holiday in St. Lucia, Marcus tries to interest Liam in beautiful local tour guide Crescentia St. Ives. Then Marcus gets stranded with Crescentia and the plot to match her with his brother quickly incinerates in the flames of lust. No way can Liam have her when Marcus can't keep his hands off. Too bad he can't write a happier ending to their blossoming romance.

Played by the Billionaire

Internet security billionaire, Liam Manning, made a promise to his beloved brother, Marcus, to complete his mystery-romance manuscript. Problem is that Liam's experience with women is limited to the cold-hearted supermodels he usually dates. So falling back on his hacking skills, he infiltrates an online dating site to find a suitable woman to teach him about romance—regular guy style. What he didn't expect was for the feelings to be so…real. Can Liam finish the novel before Lorelei discovers his deceptions and, more critically, before she breaches the firewall around his heart?

His Billion-Dollar Dilemma

Simon Lamont is an ice-cold corporate pirate. But when he arrives in San Francisco to acquire a floundering company and is accosted by a cute engineer with fire in her eyes, it takes all Simon has to maintain his legendary cool. Helen will do whatever it takes to change his mind, and if that means becoming the sexy woman Simon didn't know he wanted, so be it. If only she wasn't about to walk into her own trap...

Masquerading with the Billionaire
World-renowned jewelry designer Remington Wolfe is competing for the commission of a lifetime and someone is trying to destroy his company from the inside. He's in for more than one surprise when his unexpected rescuer turns out to be a sexy computer specialist with a sharp tongue and even sharper mind.

Romance and Intrigue in the Greek Islands:

The Greek's Stowaway Bride
Hoping to make it to North Africa to free her uncle, Rania Ghalli stows away on the yacht of Greek millionaire Demetri Christodoulou. But when Egyptian agents board the boat, she can either jump overboard...or claim she's Demetri's new bride. Demetri needs a wife to complete a land purchase so he agrees to play along—if she'll agree to a real marriage. But keeping the vivacious woman out of his heart will be a lot harder than keeping her on his ship...

An Inconvenient Series:

An Inconvenient Love
With the Italian economy in ruins, Luca Castellioni can't afford a distraction from running his

successful property restoration company. However, he needs an English-speaking wife to cement a crucial deal. When his British bride-of-convenience undermines the foundations around his heart, he's forced to restructure his priorities. Is he too late for love?

An Inconvenient Desire

Investment banker Jonathan Davis retreats to his Italian villa to lick his wounds post divorce, so his flirtation with runway model Olivia Chapman is just that. But when his ex dumps their toddler daughter on his doorstep, Olivia's assistance is a godsend that shakes up his world in more ways than one.

Canadian Romance:

Her Faux Fiancé

Take one fake engagement to a man she once loved, stir in a very real pregnancy, add a marriage of convenience, bake in the heat of revenge and you get the mess that has become Analise's life.

Business Trip Romance:

Singapore Fling

Lalita Evans's father hired Jeremy Lakewood in the family's international conglomerate, and now he's tagging along as she oversees their interests across eight countries in three weeks. Will Jeremy risk his livelihood and all the success he's achieved to win the woman who haunts his dreams?